JUST ONE STEP

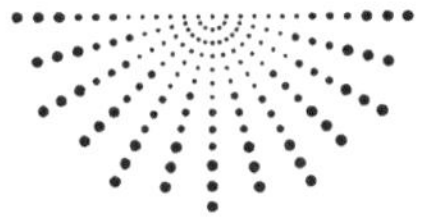

ROSIE CHAPEL

ROSIECHAPEL.COM

JUST ONE STEP

Rosie Chapel

First printing 2019

ISBN: 978-0-6485283-6-4

Ulfire Pty. Ltd.
P.O. Box 1481
South Perth
WA 6951
Australia

www.rosiechapel.com

Cover Designed by Lisa Miller with Got You Covered

NB: This novella was originally published as part of the Tempting Fate Charity Anthology under the title *Finally Home*.

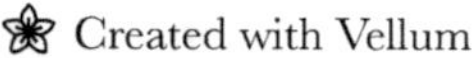 Created with Vellum

CHAPTER ONE

The sound of screaming metal seemed forever etched into her brain. No matter how hard she tried, it refused to be silenced; a constant reminder, as though she could ever forget. The terrible noise swirled around her head during the day and stalked her dreams. Six weeks after the accident it was as loud as the day it happened.

The day she lost everything.

Daisy Forrester fisted her hands, banging them hard against her stupid, useless legs. Why hadn't she been killed that day? She might as well have been — what use was she now? Not even her doctors could make it better; 'I'm so sorry Mrs Forrester, the damage to your spine may be too severe.' 'Until the swelling goes down, Mrs Forrester, we cannot tell whether you will regain the use of your legs.' On and on and on they talked, trying to sound positive, when all they meant was — well yes, we know this sucks, but them's the breaks, deal with it. No — that wasn't fair, she'd received the best of care, including daily consultations with a counsellor, who was quite lovely but, in the end, it was down to her.

To fight or to give up was solely her responsibility.

~

Her mind drifted back to that late February afternoon. The afternoon when for the first time in months she was happy. She had some exciting news and she was on holiday. They were motoring down to Cornwall, the first break they'd shared in over three years.

Micah, her husband, was often away, he flew all over the world attending conferences, but Daisy never accompanied him. He had dissuaded her, saying it was pointless; she would be bored, there'd be nothing to do while he was in sessions, and the hotels were miles from anything interesting. He stopped pretending his reasons were purely altruistic, after she caught him in an affair following a convention the year after they were married.

She had ranted and raved at him, demanding a divorce. He convinced her it was a mistake, just one of those things. At the time she was gullible and trusting, so they made up. Their fiery passion, as always, blurring her common sense. They stayed married, and he continued to attend conferences. She did not go with him and he still had affairs. They no longer mentioned it, it was like an itch he had to scratch, and he always came home to her. He obviously felt guilty, because he never failed to bring her an expensive, shame induced, gift.

Daisy's best friend, Reagan — the only person who knew — had told her countless times to kick him out, and maybe she was right, but Daisy loved Micah, faults, and all. She had loved him since they first met eight years ago, when she was seventeen and he twenty-one. He was the one who chased her, and she hadn't given in easily, wanting to be sure he was serious. He worked hard to convince her, and at the time she believed he wanted forever.

When he was with her, he was considerate, loving and attentive and, as far as she knew, he never played around close to home. The odd times Daisy forced herself to consider her situation dispassionately, she conceded she was being an idiot. Micah was a serial offender but, when push came to shove, Daisy could not bear the thought of seeing him with her replacement and, affairs aside, she believed they were as content as most married couples she knew.

The morning they set off on holiday, Daisy had received confirmation she was about two months pregnant. She suspected as much, two home tests were probably a reliable indicator, but she wasn't prepared to assume anything until her doctor verified her supposition. Although, she and Micah hadn't talked about starting a family, they had been married five years and — as everyone insisted on telling her over and over again — her body clock was ticking.

They had left home early. The roads weren't too busy, and they reached the borders of the Cotswolds just after midday. Following a tasty pub lunch, Micah took the wheel. They had only been back on the road about an hour when Daisy, who initially intended to wait until they arrived, could hold it in no longer. Excitedly, she shared her news only to see Micah's face darken, while the words spewing out of his mouth fractured her heart.

"What the hell, Daisy? How could you do this to me? You know I hate kids. What makes you think I'd ever want some obnoxious brat hanging off me, puking all over, leaving its toys everywhere, making a mess."

Daisy gawked at him in shock. "Since when do you hate kids? You have a great time playing with your nephews," referring to his sister's two boys who always dragged Micah into endless games whenever they visited. Micah never complained, throwing himself into the fun with enthusiasm.

"I can leave them when I've had enough, you don't have that luxury when you have your own. They're with you all day, every day." Micah shuddered in disgust. "You'll just have to get rid of it."

Daisy was rendered speechless. His words bounced around her head and it took several moments for his demand to register. She took a deep breath. "You want me to have an abortion?" Her voice was steady, but anyone with an ounce of sensitivity would have recognised the edge to it. Sadly, Micah was not one of those people.

"Yes, and the sooner the better, before you get attached to it."

He kept calling their baby an 'it.' Something flipped at the back of Daisy's brain and as the shutters dropped from her eyes, long suppressed anger and resentment boiled up. Generally easy going and sunny natured, it took a lot to rile her and, she had learned to control her volatile temper — characteristic of her red hair — years ago. Yelling and throwing things never worked with Micah, he just ignored her until she calmed down, then tried to discuss the matter rationally.

This, however, wasn't temper, this was icy fury. Like a dam breaking, everything she had put up with over the last few years flooded in. The *one* time something wonderful might come from what, she suddenly realised, was their sham of a marriage, he wanted her to destroy it. How stupid could she have been? Reagan was right, she was living in lala land. Micah did not give a toss about her, or their life together — it was all about him.

"Let me get this straight. You are happy to screw me, without any protection, often straight from your latest conquest. You swear you love me, and want a life together, despite your inability to keep your dick in your pants whenever I'm out of sight. Then, the minute I tell you I'm expecting a baby, a child created by you and me, a human being who deserves a life just as much as everyone else, you demand I get rid of it?" Daisy tried to control her rage, but it was unstoppable, everything she had so diligently concealed under her well-practiced veneer of marital bliss, exploded. She shrieked like a banshee until finally Micah snapped and roared back, informing her the reason he slept around was because she was frigid, boring, staid, a useless cook, all-in-all a fairly average wife, and he could not for the life of him remember why he married her.

Daisy was stunned into silence, for — all rational arguments to the contrary — she believed, underneath his crap, he loved her.

Bawling cruel insults, Micah didn't notice she'd stopped yelling. His concentration slipped, and he took a corner too fast, veering towards an oncoming truck. In an attempt to avoid a collision, Micah, still cursing up a storm, yanked the steering wheel in the opposite direction, hoping to counteract the swerve.

This was the last thing Daisy remembered with any clarity. She had a hazy recollection of the car skidding on some gravel at the side of the road and the awful sound of grinding, twisting, splintering metal, shattering glass, and the endless screaming, so much screaming.

After that it was a complete blank, which was probably a good thing. When the police interviewed Daisy later, they informed her — according to eyewitnesses — the vehicle rolled several times coming to rest on its roof at the bottom of an embankment. Thankfully, they weren't far from a large town and the emergency services arrived on scene quickly.

Unfortunately, Micah died before help reached them, leaving Daisy critically injured.

CHAPTER TWO

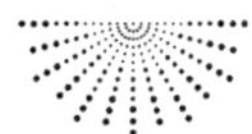

*D*aisy — trapped in the wreckage, a sizeable shard of metal lodged in her spine — had to be cut free. She also suffered serious abdominal injuries, not to mention a multitude of cuts and abrasions. When the medical team deemed her stable enough, they broke the news her baby did not survive the impact and, regrettably, while she was in surgery, they had no alternative but to perform an emergency hysterectomy, otherwise she would have bled out.

It took Daisy almost a week to comprehend this, and her doctors became concerned she was succumbing to shock, her brain simply refusing to process what had happened. During this time, Daisy underwent two more operations to investigate further, the damage to her spinal cord. Eventually, the surgeon was satisfied he had done all he could. There was nothing left to do but wait.

The day Daisy registered not only had she lost her husband, her baby, and any chance of having children in the future, but also had no feeling in her legs, was the day she had a complete meltdown. Her grief manifested in a tantrum of epic proportions, after which, she was consumed by a bout of sobbing she thought might never end. The hospital staff was incredible, such reactions were common, allowing Daisy the time needed to get it out of her system, while keeping an eye on her. When, however, it seemed as though hysteria was taking over, they stepped in, calming her down, and eventually administered a sedative. The counsellor spent hours with her, explaining the diagnosis, what her options were, and where to go from here, putting as positive a spin on everything as was humanly possible.

That was five weeks ago and, finally, Daisy believed she was beginning to come to terms with everything. It was a slow process; she continued to have good and bad days. This was a bad day. Nothing went right. She struggled during her therapy session, everything was too hard, and her upper body felt as though she'd been in a boxing match. The problem was, being essentially bed-ridden, left her too much time to think. All those years with Micah and what did she have to show for it? The more she thought about it, the more she had to admit Micah had been steadily crushing the life out of her. She acquiesced to his every whim and was stupid enough to let him have his cake and eat it.

What a pathetic excuse for a woman! She had become everything she despised, and never believed she was — a docile, gullible, subservient wife. She thought she was strong; she was the wife who loved her husband enough to see past his flaws, enormous though they were, and forgive him. In reality she was a doormat. How had she let that happen? She used to be so feisty and independent. Is that what love did to you? Turn you into a pliable automaton who accepted lies and excuses without question.

Staring out of her window onto the pretty hospital garden, Daisy wondered what the point was. Why was she bothering? Who would want her now? She was a shell of who she had been and, in all honesty, when she looked back over the last five — no eight — years, she didn't much like herself, so why should anyone else?

Had Daisy but known it, her chaotic mood swings and emotional upheaval were typical of anyone who suffered this kind of trauma. Hers exacerbated by the overwhelming sorrow at the double loss of her baby and her husband — the latter whom, whether he deserved it or not, she had loved — along with the realisation her marriage was falling apart almost before it began. Wise to this, her doctor was hoping to persuade her that now she no longer required around the clock monitoring, it would be a good idea to start planning a holiday, preferably as far from this hospital and her tormented memories as possible. Daisy would not be ready to travel for several months, but it would give her something to think about other than her current limitations.

During one of his routine visits to check on her, the doctor, almost as an aside, introduced the idea of a trip, unwittingly setting in motion Daisy's salvation.

∽

Six Months Later ~ Italy

Finally, the weather was cooler, for which Daisy was thankful. She arrived in Rome at the end of September and, until today, it had been unseasonably warm. Probably not the best destination in the world to visit when you have to explore it in a wheelchair, but Daisy was adamant. All her life she dreamed of seeing the Eternal City and, since she was no longer answerable to anyone, that was precisely where she would go. She had spent the previous two weeks doing her best to visit everything on her wish-list.

A few proved too difficult to access but most, Daisy was able to see some of, even if all that meant was steering her wheel-chair to a vantage point where she could soak in as much as possible without needing to be pushed around the whole site. Relying on others was not something Daisy found easy, but reluctantly accepted it was the only way she could manage.

When researching the trip, she came across a travel company who specialised in assisting those with all manner of disabilities, and their service was exceptional. Basilicas and churches were quite easy, large doorways and tiled or marble floors, no hindrance to a wheelchair. It was the archaeological sites, which proved the greatest challenge, and the places Daisy was most desperate to see.

Funnily enough, it was being thwarted in her attempts to tour the Roman Forum, which fired her determination to walk again. A scan, eight weeks after the accident, indicated that while the shard of metal had indeed damaged one of her verte-brae, the resultant trauma was not as dire as first suspected. Her loss of function was related to residual swelling and massive bruising, rather than severed nerves and broken bones.

Recently, Daisy had begun to experience a peculiar sensa-tion in her feet — the only way she could describe it was that it resembled the effervescence in champagne. She hadn't mentioned it to anyone, fearing she was imagining things, but the feeling had progressed to her calves, prompting a tiny glimmer of hope.

As with all spinal patients, Daisy underwent countless hours of physiotherapy and rehabilitation, acknowledging the stren-uous regimen took her mind off anything else, which might be bothering her. She left hospital with a lever-arch file full of exercises, detailed instructions on how to build up muscle strength in her limbs, how to ensure her blood was circulating properly, and how to recognise when something was amiss. The worst part was, because Daisy couldn't feel her legs, she might bang or cut them and remain unaware. Daisy was a smart woman, however, and paid attention to such things.

A battery of tests and scans revealed her liver, kidneys, and bowel, all functioned normally. The numbness was relegated to her legs only. Not particularly great news but, by that stage, Daisy was thankful for any mercy, however small it might be.

If she could take one step… just one, perhaps there was a chance of one more!

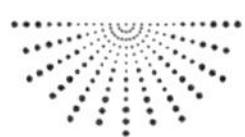

CHAPTER THREE

*H*er discovery of Rome complete, for now, Daisy was travelling to Pompeii, or rather a hotel on the bay of Naples, not far from the little Italian town and its ancient ruin. She had found a hotel advertising wheelchair access, and better still, there was a medical centre nearby. Not that she expected to need it, but it was comforting to know, so far from home, help was readily available should she experience any problems or setbacks.

Daisy booked for two months, with an option to extend. It was an indulgence, but she reasoned, since she had nothing and no one to hurry back for — why not?

The journey took a little over three hours, through glorious countryside, the colours of which were beginning to change as autumn stole away the last breath of summer. Upon her arrival at the hotel, Daisy was informed every guest with any form of disability was allocated an assistant to help with specific requirements. Seemingly, this resort often hosted sports people who were recuperating from injury or surgery, in the main because of their outstanding facilities. This also accounted for the adjacent medical centre.

After checking in, Daisy was escorted — by Flavia, her assistant — to a private villa, which was everything a person in her situation, might need. Large doorways, smooth floors, no thresholds, and solid, waist-level rails along every wall. The working surfaces in the little kitchenette and the vanity unit in the bathroom had been designed with wheelchair reliant guests in mind. All the handles were lowered, and there were no high storage cupboards. Wonder of wonders, in the spacious bathroom, there was a shower she could wheel herself into, with a seat built into the wall on which she would be able to sit to wash herself. A luxury, Daisy was ridiculously excited about.

Floor to ceiling windows ran the length of the villa, overlooking a beautifully tended garden, and beyond to the bay. Sunlight sparkled across the water, and Daisy spotted a few yachts bobbing on the tranquil sea. The air was clean and fresh with just a hint of a chill. Daisy sighed, and it seemed to come from her very soul, this was absolute perfection.

To Daisy's relief, Flavia spoke excellent English and explained everything while she showed her through the villa.

"Meals can be delivered to your room or we have a lovely restaurant just behind reception should you fancy some company."

Daisy bit her lip, eating alone was one thing she continued to struggle with. She was so used to having Micah with her, or Reagan — sitting on her own in a room full of couples and families was quite a trial.

Flavia noticed her expression and added comfortingly, "Do not fret about being alone, miss, there are plenty who prefer it that way. Trust me you would not be the only one, if you feel up to it."

Daisy smiled. "Please call me Daisy, and thank you, Flavia,

I'll give it a try. It's time I stopped moping around and hiding away. If I end up like this for the rest of my life I have to learn to deal with things. You have a lovely name by the way — very ancient."

Flavia grinned, "My father loves the classics. We all have names that sound as though we have just walked out of Virgil or Tacitus. It used to annoy me, but I'm used to it now and it is nice to be different. Like Daisy, how lucky to be named for a flower."

"Hmmm, daisies are often considered weeds or at least a pest, sprouting up all over lawns to the annoyance of the proud gardener — not that lucky," Daisy replied, ruefully.

"Oh no, daisies are beautiful. Delicate white petals and a bright yellow centre, always bobbing cheerfully. I think they are the happiest of flowers."

Daisy stared at Flavia; she had never looked at it that way. She had always been teased about her name, even Micah laughed when he was first introduced to her. She grimaced. She ought to have known right then he would turn out to be a dickhead. Shoving those thoughts aside, she thanked Flavia who confirmed she would come back at six to take her along to the restaurant.

"I know you're perfectly capable, but just for tonight, and I can show you the short cut." She winked, leaving Daisy to relax and settle in.

Before unpacking her clothes and tidying everything away, Daisy explored what would be her home for the next couple of months. Once satisfied she had created some semblance of order, she worked on her exercises. Then, using the kitchen bench top for leverage, she managed to take five steps.

Five! Not just one… *five!*

Her feet still refused to follow her bidding and she had to sort of fling her hips to make her legs go in the direction she wanted, but she was elated with her efforts. Although taking so few steps left her trembling, Daisy was triumphant. Perhaps she had a chance, perhaps she could do this. As she flopped down into her chair and looked out of the window at a sky morphing though a rainbow of colours, Daisy, to her surprise, realised she was content.

~

Daisy spent the first week becoming familiar with her immediate surroundings. She took great delight in wheeling herself along to the local café, where she treated herself to a coffee and a mouth-watering pastry or tried a different flavour of gelato — of which there were many and each one sublime. She also decided to learn Italian. Daisy loved listening to the language, its lilt touched something in her musically inclined brain and, while acknowledging her time in Italy was finite, she was determined to master it. She broached the topic with Flavia, asking what she would suggest. Her friendly assistant downloaded a program from some website or other and printed off the reasonably sized booklet which accompanied it. She also promised to help by speaking Italian and correcting Daisy's pronunciation.

Almost eight months since the accident, Daisy still tired easily, and split her day into three. Mornings were spent exploring, after lunch she would rest, before doing her exercises, and in the evening — once dinner was over — she learnt Italian.

As her first week at the hotel came to a close, she had persuaded most of the staff to help, asking them to speak only Italian with her, even if she got it horribly wrong, which was most of the time. Her mistakes reduced them to gales of laughter, but she was beginning to grasp the basics, and when she got something right her radiant smile was all the thanks they needed.

· · ·

By the beginning of her second week, Daisy was chomping at the bit to get to Pompeii. The mere name of the ruin enchanted her, and she read everything about it she could get her hands on. Accepting it might be difficult to wheel herself around, Daisy studied the map, believing if she did it in several stages, she ought to be able to see enough to satisfy herself.

The hotel provided a car, which dropped her off at the entrance near the amphitheatre. Flavia had explained the path into the ruin was relatively flat and wide, and getting into the amphitheatre itself should be a simple matter of following the tunnel. For almost the first time since her accident, Daisy was by herself, which although scary, was also liberating. Yes, occasionally she might have to ask for some assistance, but that was a small price to pay.

Excited now, Daisy paid for her ticket and trundled through the gate along the path towards the imposing grey structure, noticing the Palaestra at the left-hand side as she approached. A quick glance suggested she could probably get in there as well, but it would have to wait, the amphitheatre called to her.

She turned the wheelchair onto the ancient stones and, a few minutes of tricky negotiating later, came out into the huge circular arena.

CHAPTER FOUR

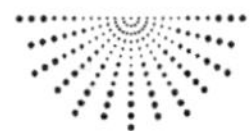

There was no one else in the amphitheatre, and Daisy
relished the solitude. She knew all about gladiatorial
combat and how the seating arrangement reflected Roman
society, but for now she just wanted to soak up the serene
atmosphere, and perhaps after a little while, attempt a few
steps. It seemed appropriate here, where men fought for their
lives. The breeze ruffled the umbrella pines surrounding the
huge structure, she could hear their needles whispering. A few
birds zipped about catching the last of the summer's bugs, the
cooler days slowing their escape.

Daisy spent about twenty minutes or so taking photos and
jotting a few things in her notebook. Since her arrival in Italy,
Daisy had begun a travel diary of sorts, a continuation of
something the counsellor suggested when she was in hospital.
Write down everything, emotions, sensations, anger, happiness,
frustration — anything at all. In Rome, Daisy wanted to make
sure she remembered every detail of her holiday, so she started
this journal. It ended up not only being about the sights, but
also how she felt each day, and whether she could see any
improvement in her legs.

.   .   .

Rolling her shoulders, stretching her neck and back, Daisy was glad to see she was still on her own with no other tourists disturbing the peace. Tucking her notebook into her backpack, she wheeled herself over to the wall delineating the arena from the seating area, and a little way around from the tunnel. Gripping the weathered stone, she pulled herself up out of the chair, leaning on the wall until she got her balance.

Conscious that the ground was a little rough, Daisy was careful, counting ten steps — five out and five back. She managed more around her villa at the hotel, but this was the first time she had tried, away from all the furniture she relied on to steady her. She wished she had brought her crutches, for she believed she might have made it to the tunnel and back. Next time — oh, there would definitely be a next time! The tingling sensation in her legs was now up to her knees, and she could wiggle her toes, the dream she might someday walk again, no longer quite so distant.

Panting a little from exertion, Daisy lowered herself into the chair, reaching into her backpack for the bottle of water. After quenching her thirst, she unzipped her jacket allowing the cool air to waft over her and, closing her eyes, let nature's symphony envelop her. It would have been easy to stay there all day, but she wanted to try getting a little further.

About to move on, a noise that in no way could be attributed to a bird or a tree burst into the quiet. Opening her eyes, Daisy noticed a little girl, perhaps three or four years old, scoot into the arena. She was bubbling with laughter, in the uninhibited manner so characteristic of young children, her giggles tugging a smile from Daisy's lips.

Spotting Daisy, the little girl ran towards her,

"Mummy, Mummy, is that you?" Her high-pitched tones echoing around the ruin.

For a split second, Daisy stiffened, feeling all colour leech from her face as she questioned whether she was hallucinating, whether her grief-stricken brain had conjured up an image of the child she lost. The girl skidded to a halt in front of her, put her thumb in her mouth, and cocked her head to one side. She was way too cute: bright blue eyes under a mop of thick caramel-blonde curls framed a heart shaped face, a button nose begging to be tweaked, and pink lips currently sucking on what was, apparently, a tasty thumb. The child's pixie-like air touched something deep inside Daisy, and she blinked rapidly, still unsure whether this was an illusion. About to speak, Daisy was startled when she heard a deep voice boom from the tunnel, the unexpected sound making her and the little girl jump.

"Molly! Molly, come here. You know you shouldn't run off like that. What would I do if I lost you?"

Oh phew — Daisy's heart slowed its frantic beat — *she wasn't imagining things.*

The little girl glanced at the approaching man, then back at Daisy, saying conspiratorially, "That's Daddy."

Unable to help herself, Daisy chuckled. The child, presumably Molly, looked so earnest. "Did you run away?" she whispered, troubled by the 'Mummy' remark. Molly shook her head.

"No, I always come here first, he knows that."

"Oh, so you live in Pompeii?"

Molly nodded, importantly. "Daddy works here," she waved her arm around the amphitheatre. Daisy was bewildered, but before she could reply, the man's long lope brought him to their side.

"I do apologise for Molly. She thinks the whole site is her personal playground." He twinkled down at Daisy and his eyes, the same vivid blue as his daughter's, did peculiar things to her insides.

Ignoring it, Daisy offered a tentative smile. "Oh, please don't apologise, I'm just relieved she's real." The man raised a quizzical eyebrow, but Daisy just shook her head, "It's nothing, just my over-active imagination."

As though realising the young woman wasn't going to say any more, he changed the subject.

"Is this your first visit to Pompeii? Are you enjoying it?"

"It is and yes, but to be honest, this is as far as I've got. I understand it's not easy navigating most of the ruin in a wheelchair, and when I came into the amphitheatre there was only me, it was so peaceful, I was loath to move. I could sit here forever, listening to the voices of the past. I am sure if I stay long enough, gladiatorial combat will materialise in front of me." As the words left her mouth, Daisy groaned inwardly. *He'll think you're an idiot,* she admonished herself, *when will you learn less is more, Daisy Forrester?*

Molly's father, who towered over her, merely grinned, seemingly unfazed by her comments, his next words explaining why.

"I know what you mean. I come here every day, yet it never fails to fascinate and enthral me." He paused, feeling moved to add, for no reason he could come up with, "I'm an archaeologist, working for the government as part of their conservation and preservation program."

"How lucky could you get?" Daisy murmured. Suddenly shy, she was very much aware this strapping bloke had to look down on her, stuck in this bloody chair. She flushed, knowing plenty of others were far worse off than she, but couldn't stop herself cursing the day her faithless husband took his eyes off the road.

The man observed an array of emotions flit across the young woman's face and was visited by the most irrational desire to soothe whatever bothered her. Before he could comment further however, Daisy started to roll forward.

"Errr… anyway, I… errr… have a nice day." She shot off as fast as her wheels would turn, leaving two moderately confused people in her wake. The last thing Daisy heard as she reached the tunnel was Molly's plaintive wail —

"Why did she go, Daddy?"

Daisy was too far away to hear the man's response but, while she persevered around the ruins, the faces of both him and his little girl were never far from her thoughts.

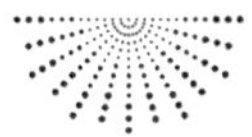

CHAPTER FIVE

*D*aisy returned to Pompeii, early the following afternoon. There was so much to see, and the previous day, she had only managed to get about two streets beyond the amphitheatre and the Palaestra, before giving up the struggle with her chair. Determined not to be beaten, her goal was the Forum. She did, however, want to try walking again, and thus headed for the amphitheatre first, hoping it was as quiet as it had been yesterday.

No such luck.

When she came out into the sunshine from the dim coolness of the tunnel, she spotted several people admiring the ancient architecture. Planning to return later to try again, Daisy spun her chair around, only to be halted by a jubilant squeal.

"Daddy, Daddy, she's here!" It was Molly and, before Daisy could hightail it, the little girl ran all the way over the grassy centre of the arena, flinging her arms around Daisy's legs.

"You came back!"

Daisy couldn't understand Molly's excitement; she had only spoken half a dozen words to her.

"Hello, Molly, how lovely to see you." She said, at the same time as she noticed Molly's father striding towards them.

"So, we meet again. We could be forgiven for thinking it was Fate," he greeted her lightly.

Daisy flicked him a suspicious glance, but his expression was bland.

"I don't believe in Fate." Her tones were harsher than she intended. Remembering her manners, she blew out her cheeks. "I'm sorry, that was churlish." Sensing an inexplicable under-current, Daisy hesitated and, in that split second, Molly's father made a decision.

"Before you rush off, may I introduce myself? My name is Adam, Adam Willoughby."

Daisy angled her head to study him, and he could almost see the debate going on in her head.

"I'm Daisy Forrester. Pleased to meet you."

Adam reached out and was gratified to feel her cool fingers slide into his. He grasped them firmly and shook, holding her gaze and her hand far longer than necessary.

Daisy was surprised to feel an unusual warmth trickle up her arm, along with the oddest notion she had been waiting her whole life for this stranger to take her hand. Shaking her head at such nonsense, Daisy gently disengaged her fingers, turning to watch Molly — who was jigging about in front of them — thankful for the distraction.

There was an awkward silence then Adam spoke, his deep voice vibrating through Daisy.

"I wonder… I know this seems a little presumptuous… but might you like to join us for coffee? Well, we could have coffee, I think Molly is hankering after an ice-cream." He smiled fondly at his daughter who beamed at him.

"Oh, Daddy, may I?" She skipped around him, singing about ice creams. Her joy in so simple a treat, infectious, and

Daisy heard herself agreeing before she had time to think about it. Manoeuvring the chair, she headed towards the tunnel. Adam walked along beside her, but didn't offer to help, for which Daisy was grateful. She had become adept at wrangling the chair over the last six months, appreciating even this small a kernel of independence.

They trundled along the Via dell'Abbondanza. Molly hopped excitedly alongside Daisy, tossing out a multitude of questions, which Daisy answered guilelessly, providing Adam with an abundance of information without him needing to ask. He wasn't sure what it was about this woman, for although they had only met twice, and for scant moments, he wanted to know everything about her.

Trying to get all the way without assistance became difficult. In spite of this, Daisy stubbornly refused to ask for help, until she nearly tipped herself out of the chair attempting to get past an uneven section.

"May I take over?" The question came so close to her ear, she could feel the warmth of his breath, and her own breathing caught.

"If it wouldn't be too inconvenient, thank you," she muttered, not altogether graciously, frustrated once more by her limitations. She studiously ignored his chuckle, keeping her attention on Molly.

Shortly thereafter, they came to the large open space, which in antiquity was the dynamic heart of the city — the Forum — currently milling with tourists, despite it being late in the year.

Adam wheeled Daisy through and over to the café, finding a convenient bench just opposite the entrance, asking whether she was happy to wait there while he organised their drinks. Nodding her head, she twisted slightly, soaking up the scene in front of her. Molly went with her father, but came back almost immediately, scrambling onto Daisy's knee.

"I'm having strawberry," she informed Daisy, "it's my very, very favourite."

"Your very, *very* favourite? Does this mean you have other favourites?"

Molly nodded, listing off at least ten more flavours, making Daisy smile. The little girl snuggled close and, without thinking, Daisy rested her chin on her head. As she inhaled the scent of Molly's baby shampoo, pesky sobs threatened. By rights, she ought to be holding her own baby now. He or she would be about a month old. She sucked in a sharp breath, then another, then a third, in a valiant attempt to get her emotions under control. Her efforts were in vain, and as Adam strolled out of the cafe carrying a tray — on which stood two steaming coffees, a plate of pastries and a tub of strawberry gelato — three fat tears escaped, rolling down her cheeks. Daisy blinked furiously, under no circumstances was she going to cry — not in front of someone she barely knew, he would think she was crackers.

Adam had noticed but made no comment. Unobtrusively, he handed Daisy a serviette, before lifting his daughter off her lap. He spent a few minutes getting Molly comfortable on the bench next to him, and ensuring she was holding her gelato properly, which allowed Daisy enough time to regain her composure. When he spoke, it was to ask some innocuous question about her holiday and by the time Daisy finished explaining about Rome and the villa, she was her usual vivacious self — almost.

Adam, however, perceived a deep-seated pain lurking in her eyes and was more determined than ever to discover its cause.

While she sipped her coffee, the rich aroma clearing her head, Daisy listened to Molly's garrulous babble, learning more from what she didn't say than what she did. It was clear the woman who gave birth to Molly was not in the picture, as the child's comments the previous day, attested. Did Adam have a girlfriend or a partner though? Was there a woman to whom he returned every evening? Did she love Molly like her own? *None of your business Daisy*, she berated herself, *seriously, what is wrong with you?* At a loss to explain the strange sadness settling over her at the thought of him with another woman, Daisy shoved it to the back of her mind, and tried to focus on the conversation, in which she was supposed to be taking part.

The afternoon slipped by while the three either sipped their drinks or, in Molly's case, slurped ice-cream, chatting as though well acquainted instead of the strangers they actually were. Daisy was thoroughly enjoying herself. It was liberating to talk to someone who had absolutely no clue who she was; she didn't have to explain or justify anything. She was also mindful the day was getting on and, glancing at her watch, realised the car would be arriving soon.

"I hate to break up the party, because this has been lovely, but I must go. I arranged for the hotel to send a car to pick me up, and it will take me a little while to get back to the gate."

"Daddy let's help Daisy," Molly interjected.

"I'll be fine Molly, you and your Daddy…"

"Of course, we'll help you, Daisy," Adam interrupted. "How do you think I would feel if your chair got stuck, or the wheel snagged on one of those cobbles and you were tipped out, because I couldn't take ten minutes to make sure you got back to the gate in one piece?"

Daisy capitulated with a shy smile. "Thank you, I appreciate it."

Adam asked Molly to drop their rubbish in the bin, while he took the tray back into the café, then the three set off towards the amphitheatre. The breeze was picking up and Daisy shivered.

"Cold?" Adam ventured

"Just a bit cool and frustrated I can't skip like Molly to warm up."

"I do like skipping," Molly piped up, "it's so much fun and you *never* get cold." Her meditative tones in complete contrast with her impish smile.

Soon they were at the gate where the car was indeed waiting. Daisy thanked Adam and Molly for sharing their afternoon.

"Will we see you again?" Molly pleaded, her lower lip beginning to wobble.

"Perhaps, it depends on lots of things." Daisy placated, unwilling to say a definite no, but also wary of extending an acquaintance with the little girl. It wasn't fair. She waved and, as the car drove away, Daisy presumed that was the last she would see of the Willoughbys.

CHAPTER SIX

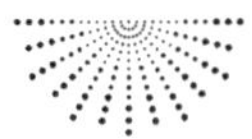

The next morning, Daisy was afforded the opportunity to visit the Naples National Archaeology Museum, and she jumped at it. She was riveted by the vast collection of artefacts, especially those from the nearby sites, but also the Greek and Renaissance exhibit. She spent a good four hours trundling around, swept up in history. By the time she returned to the hotel she was tired; confessing to Flavia that her shoulders and back ached more than usual. Flavia recommended an early night and, perhaps the next day, consider booking a hydro-therapy session, followed by a massage.

Conscious she was probably overdoing things, Daisy agreed and also resolved to curtail her explorations for the rest of the week. Following Flavia's advice, Daisy registered for hydro-therapy treatment and indulged in a deep tissue massage — finding both so beneficial, she booked one of each, every third day.

Unexpectedly, Daisy found she was looking forward to a few days' enforced rest. Since her accident, she had rediscovered the joy of reading — another pastime Micah ridiculed as boring. With her newly acquired e-reader, purchased prior to her holiday, and loaded up with a variety of novels, Daisy was easily persuaded to unwind in the beautiful hotel gardens, quickly becoming engrossed in a book.

Pompeii was never far from her mind, though and, not quite a week after she had coffee with Adam and Molly, Daisy was back at the site. As before, the hotel car dropped her off. Uncertain of how long she would be, Daisy assured the kindly driver, it would be easier if she called the hotel when ready to be picked up, instead of booking a specific time.

She managed to reach the Forum with a modicum of effort and some nifty wrangling of her chair. After exploring the areas she could access, Daisy decided a short rest was in order, unwilling to undo everything she had achieved throughout the preceding days.

Trundling to the café, she ordered a coffee and a pastry, grateful when the friendly assistant confirmed she would bring both out to her. Finding a quiet corner in the sunshine, Daisy made herself comfortable. Mere moments later, she was sipping her drink, and enjoying the opportunity to people-watch.

So absorbed was she by the bustling scene in front of her, Daisy did not see a tall man walking towards her. Nor did she hear the bell-like tones of his small daughter who was gabbling nineteen to the dozen while she jigged about alongside him, gripping his hand.

Adam's, 'Good morning, Daisy,' was drowned out by Molly's ecstatic screech when she recognised the lady in the wheelchair.

"*Daisy*!" The child's bellowed greeting echoed off the ruins, prompting several visitors to turn and stare. Their surprised expressions becoming indulgently benevolent when they spotted Molly's cherub-like face wreathed with delight.

Daisy grinned and, at the same moment, perceived an indefinable something trickling down her spine, as though her insides were smiling.

"See, I told you it was Fate." Adam smiled, and perched on a section of ruined wall next to where Daisy had parked her chair. Molly climbed onto Daisy's knee and planted a kiss on her check, before cuddling in, her head under Daisy's chin. Absently, Daisy kissed the child's curly hair and hugged her close.

"It's lovely to see you both," she said, a faint pink hue warming her cheeks. "I didn't expect to cross paths again."

"I, for one, am glad they did," Adam replied, but did not elaborate. Instead, he glanced down at Molly and asked her whether she wanted a drink or a gelato. His daughter beamed and hopped down from Daisy's lap.

"I'd better show you, Daddy." She grabbed her father's hand and dragged him towards the café.

"Would you like another coffee?" Adam queried, over his shoulder.

Daisy, amused by Molly's determined stride, nodded. "Thank you, I would love one, cappuccino please." She added, at his raised brow.

Adam nodded and let Molly lead him into the café. Before long they were gossiping over their drinks — deliciously strong coffee for the adults and apple juice for Molly. The time flew by and before Daisy knew it, coffee had become lunch — all three opting for pizza.

It was a perfect autumn day. The sun was shining, and air was mild with just a hint of a breeze wafting through the trees; Daisy could hear it rustling through the pines. Her thoughts roamed. The last few weeks had been momentous. She travelled to Italy — *on her own*, something Micah would have scoffed at. She was currently sitting in Pompeii… *Pompeii*… a place she never expected to see, and this was her third visit. Everyone she came into contact with was friendly. People offered to help if they thought she was struggling, and seemed to appreciate her attempts to speak Italian, however badly.

For the first time in longer than she could remember, Daisy became aware of a contentment, a lightness of being. Even her restrictive injuries could not dampen her simmering happiness. That it might have anything *at all* to do with the ruggedly handsome man and his adorable daughter who, apparently found her an interesting companion, she studiously refused to acknowledge… yet.

Smiling to herself, Daisy refocused on the conversation flowing around her.

Adam was asking his daughter what she wanted to do, and Molly was saying something about the Gladiators' School.

"…may Daisy come too, Daddy? I think her chair will fit."

Adam hesitated, unwilling to foist his exuberant daughter on this poor unsuspecting woman any longer.

Daisy saw it and mistook his reaction. The joyful feeling vanished.

Plastering on a smile, she said gently, "Molly, sweetheart, I have taken up so much of your time already." The little girl's face dropped as Daisy glanced at Adam, continuing, "It's okay, Adam, don't worry about me. Thank you for coffee and lunch, it has been lovely chatting. I imagine you still have a lot to see, and I will only slow you down. You, both of you, have already been very generous with your time and it wouldn't be fair for me to interfere any more in your fun." For the life cf her she couldn't prevent the chill creeping into her voice, nor the unexpected ache in her heart.

So much for Fate.

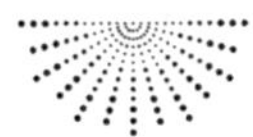

CHAPTER SEVEN

*D*aisy's feigned smile and the desolation she was not quite able to hide, elicited a curious pinching sensation in Adam's chest.

"Daisy," his tone bore a trace of gentle reproach, "I hesitated, because I don't want to inflict my overly excitable daughter onto you when we've barely met. She can be a handful. I'd be delighted if you came with us, I enjoy showing people around."

Realising she'd leapt to conclusions, Daisy felt heat wash up her cheeks, and bit her lip in embarrassment.

"I… err… well that is…" She faltered.

"Pleeeeeeeease, Daisy, pleeeeeeeease." Molly begged, putting her head on Daisy's knee and pouting in the most adorable fashion, her childish entreaty making Daisy smile. Ignoring the many, *many* warning bells clanging in her head, she gave in, saying she would love to accompany them.

Molly clapped her chubby little hands in glee, jumping about until her father suggested Daisy might not be used to such wild enthusiasm, and perhaps she ought to calm down before her new friend changed her mind.

Molly studied her father, trying to decide whether he was serious. She came to the conclusion he must be teasing. Who didn't like to jump about, and who wouldn't want to be with her?

"Daddy…" she chortled, "…you are funny. Everyone likes to jump."

Daisy burst out laughing, as a comical image of Adam jumping around Pompeii with his daughter popped into her head.

Adam was riveted when Daisy's head fell back, wayward, flaming-auburn curls spilling over her shoulders, the golden sound of her merriment rippling around them. When he looked back on it later, having known Daisy for a grand total of about four hours spread across three encounters, Adam acknowledged this was the precise moment he fell in love.

After, returning the tray, stacked with their plates and cups to the café, Adam made sure they gathered their things, and the three set off towards the Gladiators' School.

"Molly seems to know a lot about the ruins for one so young." Daisy ventured while they made their way through the throng of people.

"She's been coming with me since I started working here two years ago. She seems to love it as much as I do, and I admit to encouraging her. She's just started pre-school, but this is a holiday week. Doesn't matter what else I suggest; she just wants to come here." He smiled, watching the little girl who was skipping along ahead of them. "Careful you don't trip on those stones," he called to his daughter, receiving a wave in response.

"I think it's wonderful she wants to be with you, and how

marvellous to learn all about the history of this place almost by osmosis. I expect she will follow in your footsteps, becoming a world-renowned archaeologist."

Adam chuckled, "It'd be nice to think so, but there's nothing renowned about me," he countered modestly.

"Oh, I think you'll find there is," Daisy murmured, so quietly, Adam thought he had misheard. Unwilling to pursue it, he changed the subject, and moments later, with a little help, Daisy found herself inside the ancient school where gladiators lived or were held.

Even in its damaged state, it was imposing, and she listened attentively as Adam described the layout. He explained, in antiquity, there was an upper level, and not all gladiators were captives or slaves — there who those who chose the life, for success in combat brought celebrity.

Despite the fact Daisy knew something of the history of these gladiators, she didn't want to tell Adam, content to listen to him all day, the rich timbre of his voice enveloping her. While he was pointing out things of interest, she took the opportunity to study him. He was, in her opinion, drop-dead gorgeous. His height, as she had already noticed, easily topped six feet, and he had an athletic build. His tanned features were craggy, with a faintly weather-beaten look, which Daisy surmised was probably typical for archaeologists. His dark-blond hair, so like Molly's, was short but a bit shaggy, and abso-lutely demanded someone entangle their fingers through it.

Daisy gulped when she pictured herself doing just that. Thankfully, Adam did not appear to have heard, so she pretended it hadn't happened, and tried to concentrate. Her gaze drifted to his blue eyes, sparkling with enthusiasm as he talked — his love of this place like an aura around him — then down to his sensual lips, not too thin not too full, in fact they were the most kissable lips she'd ever seen.

For the hundredth time since she met Adam, Daisy felt her cheeks redden. Honestly, she was hopeless. She'd only known him a matter of hours, never mind she was supposed to be a grieving widow for heaven's sake. Bending her head so Adam wouldn't see, Daisy dug in her backpack, ostensibly to find her water bottle. By the time she'd taken a long draught, her equilibrium was somewhat restored, and she focused on what Adam was saying. Unfortunately, all that did was draw her attention back to his mouth, so she looked away, out over the square where gladiators once trained.

Adam, who felt he had talked long enough, said to yell out if she had any questions, and asked whether she needed help to explore.

Daisy smiled her thanks and assured him she could manage, slowly wheeling along the surrounding pathway, admiring the many columns, and peering into what would have been the gladiators' cells.

Grabbing her camera, Daisy snapped away, capturing several of the school as well as Molly and Adam. She was sensible enough to realise how improbable it was to keep meeting like this and wanted something more tangible than memories to look back on. Daisy watched Molly run the full length of the training ground, hurling herself at her father who lifted her up, twirling her around, and around making her shriek with laughter.

It was too much. Everything Daisy had lost surged to the forefront of her mind, threatening to overwhelm her, and she couldn't bear it. While the other two were messing about, their mirth echoing around the ruin, she fled, rolling as fast as she was able out onto the street, heading for the Via Stabiana which connected to the road leading to the amphitheatre. Tears pouring down her face, Daisy could scarcely see where she was going, but pushed on, desperate to get as far away as possible from such unconditional love.

· · ·

A voice called out. Daisy ignored it and forced her arms to pump the wheels faster. She hurtled along the road much too quickly for the conditions — ancient streets and wheelchairs are not a good mix. At the end of the Viale della Ginestre, the gravel gave way to the broad flag stones typical of Roman roads. Too late, Daisy spotted the line of raised cobbles. She tried to swerve but her front wheel hit the first one, upending the chair.

The last thing she heard was someone shouting her name.

She was being hurled around in a metal box — faster and faster, making her head spin. Was she at a fairground? Was this some weird carnival ride? She hated carnival rides. She needed it to stop… oh God, make it stop. She shouted for help, but the noise drowned her voice. She desperately tried to find a way out but was being thrown about too violently and she kept banging her head, in fact, she kept banging everything, and still the box tumbled. It must be a ride; it was the only explanation. What else could possibly revolve for so long?

Just when she thought this ride, or whatever it was, couldn't get any worse, Daisy felt the most excruciating pain slice through her back. Nausea threatened. Something sticky and wet ran down her face. She swiped it away, but it continued to dribble over her eyes.

The box slammed to a stop, and she tried to catch her breath — thank goodness — worst ride ever. She tried to unfold her legs from under her, but they wouldn't move, she couldn't feel them, and then something dropped into her line of sight. It was Micah, his face shredded, blood spurting out from a jagged gash across his chest. Was it his blood on her face?

Daisy fought to get out, to get away but couldn't, and she started to scream.

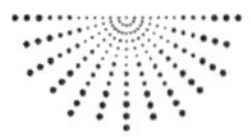

CHAPTER EIGHT

"*D*aisy, Daisy, hush sweetheart, you're ok, you're safe. Shhhhhh."

She felt herself being rocked. A deep, vaguely familiar, voice wrapped itself around her, as comforting as the arms in which she was enfolded. What on earth was going on? Where was she? Daisy didn't want to open her eyes, terrified of what she might see. She felt another scream clawing at her throat and tried to swallow it, but it gurgled up as a strangled moan, and the gentle rocking resumed.

"Daisy, please open your eyes, the ambulance is here."

Ambulance? She didn't want an ambulance, remembering what that entailed, the last time.

"Noooooo. Noooooo." She struggled, trying to disentangle herself from the arms wrapped around her, memory flooding back. "No ambulance."

"You need to let them check you over, love. You took a nasty fall."

Tell me something I don't know, she grumbled to herself — *way to look like a total idiot* — and who was calling her 'love'?

Other voices were talking over her, mostly in Italian, and the person holding her replied in the same language. Daisy picked up some of their words, 'injury,' 'back,' 'hospital,' and something about examining her head, but they were speaking fast, and she couldn't follow what they were saying. Reluctantly, she opened her eyes, recognising Adam's chin, sporting a shadow of stubble, above her. Beyond him, were two paramedics, one of whom was checking her vitals, while Adam was discussing what happened, with both of them. Daisy wriggled but Adam simply tightened his hold and continued to talk over her. She could hear sniffling and, cautiously turning her head, saw Molly scrubbing at her tear-stained face with a grubby looking hanky.

"Molly?" The little girl stared at her. "Molly, what's wrong?"

"Y-you're not dead?" The little girl stuttered.

Daisy was puzzled, unaware as soon as she spoke, everyone else stopped talking.

"No, I'm not dead, at least I don't think so. Why did you think I was dead?"

"You f-fell and you didn't m-move, that's what h-happens when you g-get deaded." Little hiccups threading through her words.

Daisy felt her heart crack — this child… "Molly, I'm fine. My wheel caught on a bit of stone, and when I fell out of the chair, I must have banged my head. I am certainly not dead."

"S-sure? You screamed t-too. It was very l-loud." Molly wasn't convinced, her bottom lip was quivering.

Daisy reached out to grasp the child's hand and draw her close. Tucking the little girl against her, she kissed her cheek.

"Positive. I'm talking, and I kissed you, and you can't do that or scream if you're dead. Here…" she placed Molly's hand on her chest. "…do you feel that?" Molly nodded. "That's my heart, if you can feel it beating, I'm alive."

Molly left her hand there for a few seconds. Then, satisfied, squeezed Daisy's face between her hands, and planted a sticky kiss on her mouth. "Good. I like you. I didn't want you to be deaded."

"I like you too, and I'm sorry I scared you with my screaming." Daisy winked, and Molly smiled shyly.

A subtle cough brought her attention back to the group of people standing around her, and the man in whose arms she lay. She tried to sit up, helped by a large hand supporting her back.

"Thank you, I didn't mean to cause trouble." Her apology, a less than intelligible mix of Italian and English. "It was my own stupid fault. I don't need an ambulance, no more ambulances…" her voice trailed off.

Adam hugged her to him. "Could you at least let them finish giving you the once over. You gave us all a bit of a fright." Daisy frowned, and he elaborated. "You were thrown from your chair and, presumably, knocked yourself unconscious, because you were so still and silent, then out of the blue, you started screaming and writhing."

She twisted to look him in the eye, his quiet words at odds with his clenched jaw and anxious expression.

"I'm sorry…" Without thinking, Daisy cupped his cheek, then realising what she'd done, snatched her hand away. "Okay, if they must." She made to stand up, then remembered she couldn't walk. *Oh hell, yeah, that minor inconvenience.* She huffed a grudging sigh and waited until one of the medics brought her chair. Before Adam could lift her into it, Daisy shuffled forward on his knee, swinging across with practised ease. The medic wheeled her along the Viale della Ginestre to a waiting ambulance, which somehow managed to drive quite a way along the ancient street.

Adam watched the paramedics take Daisy to check her over, strangely bereft without her in his arms. Her screams not only freaked out Molly, they terrified him. What on earth had happened to elicit such a reaction and what had prompted her to flee from them in the first place? Again, he struggled to comprehend why this woman made him feel so protective. Something about Daisy was yanking hard on his heartstrings, yet he knew nothing about her. The realisation, if she hadn't fallen, he might never have seen her again, left a gaping hole within him, and he couldn't shake the notion that to kiss her would be like coming home.

Adam was no lovesick boy; he was a thirty-three-year old single father, working for the conservation department of the Italian government. He had enough to do bringing up Molly on his own without the added complication of Daisy. To become involved with anyone right at this moment was too big a step. He should make sure there was no lasting damage from her fall, thank her for her company, and walk away.

Molly slipped her tiny hand into his, and Adam looked down at his daughter. She was his whole world and he wasn't prepared to compromise on that. Then he remembered how patient and kind-hearted Daisy was with her; treating Molly sensibly, speaking on a level the little girl understood without babying or cosseting her. He also recalled her muttered words when they first met in the arena... *I'm just relieved she's real.*

What did she mean by that? Daisy Forrester was quite the puzzle. Adam liked puzzles, and the thought of solving this one, sent heat coursing through his veins. Making a decision, he hoisted Molly onto his shoulders and strode along the path to the ambulance, his daughter chortling with glee, hung onto his hair while she bounced up and down.

The medics were still examining Daisy, but it couldn't have been too serious because he heard her laughing. It was that same golden sound he had heard earlier, and it was reverberating around the walls of the vehicle.

• • •

Ten minutes later, the back door of the ambulance swung open. One of the medics lifted Daisy out and into her chair.

Her brow creased in puzzlement when she saw Adam, wondering why he had bothered to wait.

While one of the medics was getting Daisy sorted out, his colleague advised Adam they could see no serious damage, but she was likely to be sore and bruised. They had examined her legs for any cuts or abrasions, finding none, but had given her a report of the incident and their findings, just in case. The three men discussed Daisy's condition in Italian, the medics assuming Adam was her husband, something from which he did not disabuse them, learning far more than he suspected Daisy would reveal.

Saying goodbye to Daisy with a "hope you feel better soon," they drove off.

Silently, Daisy waited for the censure she assumed would follow. She deserved it; the accident served her right. Her behaviour was nothing short of irresponsible. Micah would have been quick to berate her, had she acted so thoughtlessly when with him. The few occasions she walked away, during one of their arguments, he followed her, starting another argument over the fact she dared to leave him looking like an idiot.

Daisy sighed, realising for the umpteenth time since the crash, her marriage was never happy, she was blinkered the whole time. Had she ever loved Micah, or was she just in awe of him? It was clear he had never loved her, going as far as denying the passion she was certain they shared.

Adam studied Daisy, confused by the conflicting expressions chasing across her pale features. She appeared almost scared, definitely on edge. Surely, she wasn't frightened of him. He'd given her no reason to be.

"Daisy, how do you feel?"

She raised her eyes to his and he read anguish in their emerald depths.

He crouched down next to her, taking her hand, surprised to feel it trembling. "What are you afraid of?"

Daisy shook her head. She couldn't tell this man; he would walk out of her life in less than five minutes. There was no point, he didn't need her baggage.

CHAPTER NINE

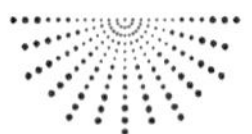

"It's nothing, honestly. It's not your concern, Adam. Thank you for today, you have no idea..." she faltered, then straightened her shoulders. "I'll call for the hotel's car. You and Molly don't need to hang around, I'm sure you've better things to do. I'll treat myself to a warm bath and try to get a good night's sleep." Withdrawing her fingers, Daisy rummaged in her bag for her phone, but before she found it, his hand once again covered hers.

"Please allow me drive you back to the villa. It's the least I could do."

Daisy frowned. "No, I couldn't let you, Adam. It's probably the opposite direction to where you live, and you have Molly to think about and—"

Adam didn't want to argue with her, and was determined to drive her home, so he did the only thing he could think of to shut her up.

He leaned close and kissed her.

As far as Daisy was concerned, time juddered to a screeching halt. When Adam's lips touched hers, it was all she could do not to haul him against her and let him kiss her senseless. She forgot everything else — where they were, the other tourists, Molly — *oh hell, Molly, he was kissing her in front of Molly.* Still she couldn't stop it. He deepened the kiss and she exhaled a soft moan, hundreds of butterflies taking flight in her stomach. Her arms went around his neck, and she plunged her fingers into his hair, surprised to find it thick and silky. He shuddered, drawing her against him, sliding her forward on the chair.

Seconds later, as Daisy was beginning to question whether the chorus of birds were singing just for her, Adam and she were disturbed by a childish giggle. They broke apart. Daisy blushed yet again, and twiddled with the toggle on her jacket zip, while Adam rubbed his hand around the back of his neck, as both strove to steady their breathing.

"Daddy, it's my turn." Molly elbowed her father out of the way, crawling onto Daisy's lap, to bestow another sticky kiss, before putting her arms around Daisy's neck, and hugging her tightly. "That's two kisses to make it all better. So, by tomorrow you'll be right as rain," she said.

Daisy smiled, recognising words her own mother used to say when she tripped — which was often. A kiss always made everything better. Well Molly wasn't wrong, that was for sure, her lips still tingling from Adam's kiss. She brought her attention back to Molly who was still talking. "If you let Daddy take you home, you can sit in my car seat. It stops you falling out of the car."

Warmed by the child's concern, Daisy dropped a kiss on the honey-coloured curls.

"Thank you, poppet. Okay, I'll let your daddy drive me home, but only if you promise to sit in your seat. I think it might be a bit small for me, and I don't want to damage it."

Molly agreed this might indeed prove to be the case, adding, "Right Daddy, time to go. Come on." Not moving from

Daisy's knee, tired after her long day and glad she could be cuddled by this nice lady, Molly waved her hand, imperiously, in her father's general direction.

Daisy heard laughter rumble through Adam's chest, and the wheelchair began to roll forward.

Fortuitously, Adam's car was parked not too far from where the ambulance had pulled up. When they reached it, he stood back, letting Daisy sort herself out presuming, correctly, she was far more used to getting in and out of cars than he was to assisting. Strapping Molly in, Adam handed his daughter a book and a teddy, by which time, Daisy had eased into the front passenger seat, and her wheelchair was already folded, ready to be stowed in the boot.

The car reflected Adam, large and powerful, and it slid noiselessly along the road as Daisy gave him the address of the hotel. Before she knew it, the purr of the engine, Molly's chitchat, and the classical aria playing on the radio had lulled her to sleep.

A hand was shaking her shoulder, and her was head lolling. *Oh lordy, had she fallen asleep in his car?* Daisy grimaced; she'd probably drooled all over his perfect leather seats too — awesome!

"Daisy we're here."

She opened her eyes blinking a little, while she tried to get her bearings. Her brow creased; this didn't look familiar.

"Molly wants you to stay for dinner." A contrite voice explained.

"Am I being kidnapped?" she accused in undertones. Adam merely shrugged his shoulders. So, it was a possibility then…!

"Pleeeeeeeease, Daisy," Molly beseeched. Daisy was putty in this child's hands; she couldn't say no, even though she knew it was a mistake. Shaking her head in resignation, she acquiesced.

"Just this once, Molly Willoughby. You two have quite enough to do without looking after me," She smiled, her tones gently chiding.

Molly didn't seem in the slightest rebuffed. "Goody!" she chirped.

Adam lifted Daisy's chair out of the boot and stood it by the front passenger door. In the few seconds it took for him to unfasten his daughter's seatbelt, Daisy had shifted across into the wheelchair.

Always leery of visiting someone else's house, Daisy was pleasantly surprised to find the Willoughby home to be large, airy, and open plan. There was plenty of room for her to manoeuvre her wheelchair and, later when she needed to use the bathroom, found she could manage without any difficulty.

Adam whipped up a simple, yet tasty pasta dish, and the three sat around a huge rustic style kitchen table, talking about all manner of things without any awkwardness. The adults had wine with their meal, after which, Adam poured Daisy a small limoncello, leaving her decidedly mellow.

Molly scampered off the minute she'd eaten and was soon engrossed in a Disney movie. Adam tidied the crockery, and stacked the dishwasher, before making Daisy and himself a hot drink. Daisy was astonished. Micah had never offered to help with the dishes, she was expected to deal with everything domestic. She supposed for Adam, being a single father, it was second nature — nevertheless it was refreshing. The two sat in companionable silence while they sipped the fragrant tea, and Daisy had never felt more welcome. Not in the home she shared with Micah, not in the home in which she grew up. How was that possible? It was as disconcerting as it was comfortable.

. . .

Without seeming to, Adam encouraged Daisy to open up, and she found herself telling him all about the accident, and her marriage, and her battle to walk again. Her determination to take that first step and how incredible it felt when she finally achieved it. She didn't mention losing the baby or that she was no longer able to have children. Such admissions were too personal and still way too raw.

Daisy was constantly amazed she could talk about Micah unemotionally, but not so the baby. It wasn't as though she had experienced being pregnant. She had only just found out, hadn't had her first scan, yet it possessed the power to unravel her. Without thinking, Daisy mentioned Molly's unnerving appeal the first day they met. Ruefully, Adam assured her it was just his daughter's latest fixation, because all her friends had a mummy. He didn't go into further detail, but somehow made it clear there was no other woman in his life.

Daisy had no idea how long they'd been talking, until she glanced at the large clock on the kitchen wall — it was nearly nine.

"Oh Adam, I should call a taxi. You have Molly to organise, and I need to get back to the hotel. They probably think I'm locked inside Pompeii."

"The hotel knows you're with me. I rang them from the car."

Daisy looked confused. "How on earth did you know where to call?"

"You gave me the address, remember. I just found their number and rang them. They are a little concerned about your accident, but glad to know you're okay. Don't fret Daisy, I'll get you back safely."

Studying his face, she saw only friendly kindness, so accepted it for what it was and nodded, nestling back into the chair.

. . .

They chatted a little longer, but Adam could see Daisy was bothered about keeping him out late. Little did she realise he could have happily talked with her all night, mesmerised by her expressive features and startlingly green eyes. While her story unfolded, they changed colour constantly, darkening almost to black as she explained about the accident and coming to terms with the aftermath, then glowing with emerald fire when she mentioned the sensation in her feet and legs, and the few steps she had attempted.

"I don't know how you've done it." Adam's voice held a note of admiration, as they prepared to leave.

"I haven't done anything," she demurred, shrugging into her jacket. "There are loads of people far worse off than me. You're the only person who knows about me trying to walk. I couldn't quite believe it; afraid it was my imagination. I practise in my room at the villa, and even had a go in the amphitheatre, only because it was empty mind you."

"Maybe you would like to try again tomorrow?"

Daisy stared at him, "What… why?" she whispered, a flutter of something stirring in her chest.

"Because Molly and I would like to help you practise."

The flutter died a little.

"Ahh, yes, Molly." Her eyes fell from his. This was crazy, she couldn't do it. What was she thinking? That he was her knight in shining armour? Yeah right, like they existed. In six weeks, she would return to England or — and more likely — long before that, he would come to the conclusion it was too hard. There was Molly; Adam didn't need some woman with useless legs messing up his life. He had enough on his plate looking after his daughter. So, what if they enjoyed each other's company? It couldn't go anywhere — it *shouldn't* go anywhere. He needed someone whole and healthy, able to run and play with his daughter, and give him more children.

Anyway, why are you thinking like this, Daisy Forrester? You have known him less than twelve hours. Get over yourself.

She felt sobs building.

Oh hell — not again, she was absolutely sick of crying. Surely, she was stronger than this.

CHAPTER TEN

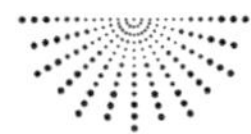

Studying her, Adam saw Daisy's face begin to crumple, and then harden as a mask dropped across her features. She was pulling away, as though physically leaving him, and he didn't think he could bear it. With an inkling of what worried her, Adam knew he had to persuade her she was wrong, that he needed her as much as she needed him and, whatever she thought, he wasn't letting her go without a fight.

"Daisy don't shut me out. I suspect I can guess what bothers you, and you cannot think much of me if you expect me to turn my back on you."

The sudden quiet, lengthened.

"You don't even know me." Doubt clear in her muttered words.

"Maybe not yet, but I wish you would give me a chance. I know we only just met, and I'm as astonished as you probably are about what seems to be happening between us. I doubt either of us expected it, but that doesn't make it any less real. Why don't we try? Why don't we see where this might lead? You trusted me enough to share your story, please let me be here for the next chapter. I don't think you'll regret it."

He paused, and then went on to clarify his idea. "How

about this. What if we get together each day? I'll help you practise walking, and you can let me show you Pompeii and Hercu-
laneum as well as the other ruins, and the Bay. You say you're
booked at the villa for another month or so?" He raised an
eyebrow and Daisy nodded. "Give us that time, and if at any
point you decide it's not what you want and…" when she
started to interrupt, "…can give me a valid reason why, I won't
argue." He reached for her hand, his thumb rubbing down
hers, the gesture recreating those delicious tingles she had experienced earlier.

"Are you sure?" she murmured, the flutter pulsing back to
life. "I'm quite broken you know."

"You're only as broken as you allow yourself to be. I don't
see a broken woman, I see a woman who's taken a bit of a
bashing and might be a bit dented, but who certainly isn't
broken."

His smile snuck under her barriers, she couldn't resist him,
and although the eminently sensible and very scared part of
her insisted she was being irrationally stupid, that this would
only lead to heartbreak, her romantic nature — bruised though
it was — ignored it, desperately hoping Adam was right.

As he leaned against the table watching her, Adam knew
what Daisy's decision was before she told him — her eloquent
face relaxed, and her eyes began to sparkle. Without giving her
time to discern his intention, he bent his head and kissed her.

Daisy had to admit, as her senses exploded in total chaos,
Adam was *the* best kisser. His lips were firm and warm when
they moved over hers, leisurely and tenderly, full of promise.
She opened to him, their tongues tangling. His hand slid
around to cup the back of her head, fingers threading through
her curly hair. Needing more, Adam scooped her from the
chair as though she weighed nothing, perching her on the
kitchen bench, tucking her legs around his hips, and moulding
her to him. Her heart was beating faster than a hummingbird's
wings, and her breathing was all wonky. Daisy whimpered

when his arms enclosed her, her head falling back as his lips trailed a scorching path down her neck to the hollow at the base of her throat. Then, as though reading her mind, his mouth recaptured hers, and they sank deeper and deeper into a swirling vortex, which threatened to undo them completely.

Daisy came back to earth first, a squeal from Molly piercing the squishy mess she now called a brain, and she drew away, breathing heavily. Adam looked as dazed as she felt, his hands stroking up and down her spine.

"I think we'd better stop," Daisy managed a husky croak, running one finger along his jaw line, the stubble rough under her fingers.

"I'm not sure I have the willpower." His voice was a similar rasp.

Daisy giggled; Adam looked totally discombobulated. "Come, on, I have to get home. I need a good night's sleep if you insist on your crazy plan. Mind, how that's achievable after your kiss is beyond me."

Adam grinned, inordinately gratified she was as affected as he. He patted her on the butt, lifting her off the bench and into her chair.

"Molly," he called, "come on sweetheart, we're taking Daisy back to her hotel."

"Can't she stay for a sleepover?" Molly petitioned when she came into the room. Adam met Daisy's eyes over his daughter's head, smothering a chuckle when she rolled her eyes.

"Maybe next time, poppet." Daisy sweetened her refusal. "I don't have my pj's or my toothbrush.

"You could wear Daddy's," came the innocent reply. By now Adam was laughing out loud at his daughter's inadvertent alignment with his own desires.

"Molly, let Daisy be," he intervened, taking pity on Daisy, who was fiery red. "Where's your coat?" He shooed his daughter off to find it, apologising for her candour.

Daisy waved it off. "It's what kids do, no biggie."

Coat found, Molly came running back along the hall while Daisy wheeled herself to the front door, and soon they were motoring through empty streets. It wasn't long at all before the car drew to a quiet halt at the front of the hotel. The doorman came out to assist, but Adam beat him to it, helping Daisy into her chair, whereupon, she thanked him for a lovely day, and even better evening.

"I'll pick you up tomorrow at eleven, and you can stay for dinner again."

Daisy started to say she would make her own way to the ruins, but Adam was having none of it.

"My idea, I'll come get you."

She nodded, smiling shyly.

Bending, Adam brushed his lips to hers, grasping her fingers, and squeezing them gently. "Until tomorrow."

He was in the car and gone before Daisy could respond.

Adam was as good as his word. He and Molly picked her up on time, driving her to Pompeii. As one of the resident archaeologists, he managed to get Daisy in without charge, and also had access to areas rarely seen by the public. Daisy was fascinated. Adam was an interesting guide, explaining each section as they toured it, but without all the technical jargon, which might be overwhelming.

The days fell into a pattern. After breakfast, Daisy did her exercises, and prepared for the day. Adam collected her and they spent a few hours at one of the ruins or visiting local beauty spots, returning to his house where she could practise walking, after which they shared the cooking. Every day, Daisy felt stronger. She was taking more and more steps, and despite knowing the road ahead was long, it didn't seem as bleak as before. Her holiday, however, was coming to an end, and the thought of not seeing Adam and Molly every day tore at her soul, something she was determined *not* to reveal to the two in question.

~

Three days before Daisy was due to leave, Molly implored her… again, to have a sleepover the following night. Adam pointed out they had a perfectly good guest room which never got used. It had a walk-in shower with a ledge running all the way around. Daisy was able to stand now while she showered but, occasionally, her legs refused to follow instructions and she wasn't confident enough to risk it without some form of support.

Molly begged and pleaded, and, against her better judgement, Daisy gave in. She was concerned, having spent so much time with the little girl, her imminent departure would be made worse if she stayed, but since Adam didn't seem perturbed, she swallowed her misgivings and packed an overnight bag, grateful she brought her cutest pj's.

CHAPTER ELEVEN

The next morning, while waiting for Adam, Daisy reflected on the last few weeks and, while she was the one with reservations, had enjoyed the days they spent together, immensely. Adam had not revisited their discussion about next chapters and Daisy, acutely aware time was running out, wasn't game to bring it up.

Adam, however, knew what he wanted; he just didn't want to pressure Daisy. He guessed there was something she wasn't yet brave enough to share, and he had his own secret. For them to have any future together, they both needed to come clean. Much as he was desperate to romance her, to love her — okay, to have her writhing naked under him, the mere thought of which sent his heart rate into overdrive — he wanted Daisy to know he trusted her with every facet of his life.

Daisy, her hard work and diligence with her exercise regimen seemingly paying off, had faith not only would she walk again, but also possibly run. Well, maybe not run exactly, she'd never been a runner, but move quickly, walk a dog, play with a child. There it was, her Achilles heel — play with a child. The only child within reach was Molly, and she wasn't her child. Daisy couldn't assume Adam had any interest in a long-term relationship. Yes, they indulged in a *lot* of kissing, but he hadn't taken it any further, despite his desire for her being obvious.

Was she kidding herself? Had she let the joy of being part of a family — even for so short a time — blind her to the reality of her situation? Micah's last words tormented her; boring, staid and useless. Adam and Molly survived her cooking so maybe Micah lied about that, but the rest of it…? Her thoughts spiralled out, and by the time Adam arrived to pick her up, at nine, the early start at his request, Daisy was completely out of sorts.

Her dark expression when she wheeled herself out to meet the car did not bode well; she was clearly chewing over something. Adam ignored it, greeting her with his usual cheerfulness. He placed her overnight bag for the promised sleepover in the boot, and soon, they were motoring along the road towards the bay. He turned onto the A3 for Naples, chatting about nothing in particular until Daisy began to look brighter, although confused as to where they were going, and why so early.

"Capri," Adam informed her when they reached the outskirts of Naples. "Now let me concentrate, it gets tricky here." The car fell silent while Adam wound his way to the airport. Parking the car, he helped Daisy, now completely bewildered, into her chair then wheeled her into the terminal. What on earth were they doing at the airport? Before long, all became clear; Adam had organised to fly them to the island by helicopter. Daisy was astounded; it must have cost him a small fortune.

"Adam," she stuttered, as he wheeled her out to the helipad. "You didn't need to do this… the cost. You're crazy!"

"My treat, and the pilot is a friend of mine who owes me a favour." He introduced Jasper, who smiled and nodded at Daisy. Adam grinned as he strapped her in, adjusting the headset so it sat snugly over her hair. "Ready?"

She nodded nervously. Adam sorted out his own straps, gave Jasper the thumbs up, and took Daisy's hand. She gripped his fingers tightly as the helicopter whirred to life, slowly lifting into the air. Daisy had never been in a helicopter and feared she might get motion sickness. No such thing, she loved it. It was an exhilarating experience, and twenty minutes later, Jasper flew over the island, pointing out the Roman villas and the Blue Grotto, making Daisy squeal like a giddy child.

Shortly thereafter, Jasper was lifting her into the back seat of a car, which drove up on their arrival. The chauffeur tipped his cap at Daisy, while he and Adam discussed something. The two men spoke in Italian; there was nodding and gesticulating, then Adam was sitting next to her, entwining their fingers, his thumb stroking hers.

They drove for about fifteen minutes, until Daisy saw a sign announcing Villa Damecuta. Adam explained this was one of twelve villas built by Emperor Tiberius and was situated directly above the Blue Grotto. The car slid quietly to a halt, and the chauffeur alighted, walking around to the boot to lift out the wheelchair. While Daisy got herself settled, Adam had another brief conversation with the driver, then asked Daisy whether she minded him pushing the chair because the ground was uneven.

"I think trying to manoeuvre the chair around the whole of the ruin might be too difficult but I'm pretty sure I'll be able to manage some of it, as well as take you to a spot where you can see the view which, I promise you, is worth every bump," he remarked. "That is if you trust me." He pulled a hideous face and waggled his eyebrows.

Daisy couldn't help but giggle at his expression. "I trust you, as long as you don't speed, and that sounds fine to me. I can try to walk a bit too, if you help me," she replied, excited to explore.

Once they were inside the site, Adam was able to wheel the chair around a fair amount of the ruin and Daisy peppered him with questions about the history of the villa. He was right, however, it was the view which took Daisy's breath away. Tiberius, who spent the last half of his reign on Capri, ensured this isolated complex was strategically positioned not only to impress, but also to make it difficult for any would-be assassins to reach him. Today it was simply a beautiful place to visit, to soak in the ancient atmosphere and admire the Bay of Naples, in all its turquoise glory, spread out in front of them.

With Adam's help, Daisy walked to the railing where she stood for a long time breathing in the refreshing, sea air.

"Why is Capri a special place?" she queried, recalling Adam's earlier comment.

"One of my favourite books is *The Story of San Michele* by Axel Munthe. In the first chapter, there's a scene which unfolds in one of Tiberius' villas here on the island. The main character, a doctor, communes with a robed figure, a shade who, among other things, talks of antiquity, of how an emperor trod the marble floors and how myriad multi-coloured frescoes once adorned the walls. It was this passage which inspired my love for ancient Rome, for archaeology. I wanted to tread those same paths, to see the frescoes, and the statues, and the mosaics — in place, not in museums." He spoke quietly, but underlying his words was that same animation, that same enthusiasm, Daisy had heard when he described the Gladiator's School all those weeks ago.

Adam shrugged and spread his palms… somewhat self-consciously, Daisy thought, endearing him to her even further… concluding, "So, that's why Capri is special."

She smiled and, using the railing for leverage, stretched up to kiss him, light as a feather. "Thank you for sharing, and now I absolutely must read the book!"

Adam hugged her to him, returning her kiss with interest. For a little longer they stood, arms round each other. Not talking, content to gaze out over the glittering sea, captivated by the incredible panorama. Eventually, Adam suggested they have lunch. Returning to the car, where the driver was waiting patiently, Adam removed a large wicker basket and two colourful rugs from the boot. After asking Daisy to nurse both, he had a word with the driver, who nodded and drove away.

Careful to avoid the many twisted roots underfoot, Adam wheeled Daisy to a secluded corner under a shady tree, away from inquisitive tourists. He laid out one of the rugs, helping Daisy to make herself comfortable, and then rolled the second rug into something resembling a bolster cushion. Standing the basket next to where Daisy was sitting, Adam raised the lid. It was full to bursting with all manner of picnic treats, including champagne.

Daisy's jaw dropped.

"What... how... did you decide... rain..." Daisy couldn't form a sentence for the life of her, so she just gawped.

Adam chuckled. "I've been arranging this for a week, made sure everything was organised and, if the weather turned, I had Plan B up my sleeve. Here..." he passed Daisy plates, serviettes and glasses. "...wow, they have done us proud." He kept handing out the beautifully packaged food until Daisy, laughingly, cried a halt.

"Stop it, Adam. I've nowhere to put any more."

Adam grinned as he twisted back around to see Daisy looking as though she was the guest in a certain Disney movie.

"We can't possibly do justice to all this," she said, unable to stop a moan of pleasure when she bit into one of the sandwiches. "Adam, you have to try these, lordy they are scrummy."

The pair feasted until Daisy declared her stomach was going to burst, and hoped he wasn't in a hurry to get back, because there was no way she could move for at least an hour. Lying back against the makeshift cushion, she stared up through the tapestry of branches to a sky so incredibly blue it was almost painful, and she closed her eyes against the brilliance — only to see the image imprinted on her lids. Autumn might be nearly over, but today the sun was warm and, tucked against a section of ruined wall, they were protected from any breeze.

Neither spoke for several minutes. Adam balanced on one elbow to study Daisy. Her flaming hair, coming loose from its usual thick plait, framed a face paler than it should be despite the two months she had been in Italy. Sensing his scrutiny, her eyes flickered open, colliding with his, blue as the sky above their heads, and something about his gaze made her wary.

"What is it, Adam?" She raised herself, so their faces almost touched. Adam drew a sharp breath and brushed his mouth over hers.

"I could kiss you 'til the end of time," he murmured.

Faint colour stole up Daisy's cheeks and her face took on a dreamy expression. "Then, why don't you?" she implored quietly, her cheeks darkening when she realised, she had said that out loud. "Oh... err... that is... I didn't... maybe not really—"

"Shhhhh," Adam interrupted her babble, rubbing his thumb over her bottom lip and on down her throat, making her tremble.

"Adam..." she whispered; her voice unsteady.

"Mmmm..." He was too distracted by the freckles scattered over her creamy skin and the pulse fluttering in her neck to hear what she was saying.

"Adam, I ... there's something you ought to know."

"In a minute." He lowered his head and kissed her, stealing her breath when she tried to speak. His fingers ghosted along her body, igniting a fire that had never quite burnt out since first he kissed her and, under his expert touch, Daisy was lost. Uncaring that they were in full view of anyone walking past, that she would be leaving in two days, or that she was about to share her last secret — one which might snap the slender thread binding them — Daisy wrapped her arms around him, pulling him on top of her, needing to feel his weight, needing to feel all of him.

Adam went willingly, his hands roaming over her slender frame, one pushing under her long-sleeved tee, gliding over her back, while the other teased under the waistline of her jeans making her squirm and arch into him. She tugged at his shirt, desperate to feel his skin. Cool, inquisitive fingers tracing the hard planes of his muscular physique. Adam groaned, her tentative exploration undermining his self-control.

"Oh God, Adam, please… I… arghhh…"

His relentless fingers finally undid the button and opened the zip, seeking her centre beneath the wispy triangle of silky material. Daisy shuddered, nothing in her life, in her marriage, prepared her for the mind-blowing sensations crashing through her. Just when she thought she was going to shatter, he eased away letting her catch her breath only to spark another blaze when his fingers tiptoed under her tee again. He pushed it aside, trailing kisses across her now hypersensitive skin, creating wave upon wave of delicious tingles.

Daisy couldn't think, couldn't breathe, her whole being consumed by white light.

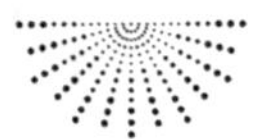# CHAPTER TWELVE

$\mathcal{A}$dam knew he had to stop this madness. He didn't want to, he never wanted to let Daisy go, but he had a secret. While revealing it ought not to affect their relationship, she deserved to know, to have all the facts before she took one more step, the step he hoped would bring her to his side forever.

"Daisy." He lifted his head from his tortuous journey over her heated body. "First, while I desperately want to continue this, I prefer to do so elsewhere." He dropped a slow and lascivious wink, making Daisy blush — again — honestly, she was worse than a teenager. "Second, I must tell you about Molly." Seeing anxiety in the azure depths of his eyes, Daisy nodded, shuffling back up onto the cushion, straightening her clothes, while Adam did the same. Moving the rolled rug against the wall giving them something to lean against, he stretched out his legs, lifting her onto his lap and anchoring her to him, his cheek resting on her head.

"Where to start." He heaved a sigh. "Molly isn't my daughter." Shocked, Daisy twisted to face him. Adam smiled a little sadly. "Well, yes she is, to all intents and purposes. She's my twin sister's child, born just over four years ago to a mother already dead."

Daisy sucked in a sharp breath, and began shaking her head — *oh God, no.*

"Nina, my sister, died of a heroin overdose, but the doctors were able to save Molly. She went through withdrawals and for a while was seriously ill, but she's fine now, a normal four-year-old with no residual issues. They were concerned about cognitive development, but by some miracle she suffered no adverse effects. I had no idea Nina was pregnant, or who Molly's blood father was. I hadn't seen my sister for over three years; she just dropped off the radar. Social services contacted me when they found my details on a scrap of paper in Nina's purse. As her only remaining family member — my parents are dead — I was allowed to adopt Molly, and she is the most important person in my life. At least she was until about two months ago, when a red-haired beauty stole my heart."

Daisy's head snapped up and she stared at Adam. His expression was one of trepidation with just a hint of hope.

"What are you saying, Adam?"

"I'm saying I love you. I've been in love with you since our second coffee in the Forum." Pressing a kiss on her forehead, he cradled her against him once more, interlocking his hands across her stomach. Daisy was silent for so long, Adam worried he'd blown it. Then, she stroked her hands over his, before lifting one, and kissing his knuckles. His tension abated a little.

"There is something I must tell you too, I should have done sooner, especially in light of what you've just said," she began.

Adam experienced a flicker of unease, Daisy sounded oddly resigned. He held his tongue, waiting.

"On the day of the accident, I'd just told Micah I was pregnant. We'd been married five years, I thought he'd be excited." She paused, and swallowed her rising grief. "He told me to abort it, he actually called our unborn child an it." Daisy felt Adam's arms tighten around her. Grabbing her courage in both hands, she told him everything Micah said, about having children, about how useless she was, her lack of sexuality, that he couldn't remember why he'd married her — everything. She blurted it out far too rapidly for complete comprehension, but Adam worked it out. Finally, she told him about losing the baby and having a hysterectomy.

"So, you see, when I thought Molly was your daughter, I dared to hope, because you already have one child, perhaps you don't need any more. I can't give you a child of your blood. I am little more than a husk and apparently not that good at being a wife or sex anyway, what could you possibly want with me?"

Silently, Adam cursed Micah from Italy to England and back again for the damage he'd done to Daisy both physically and mentally. Although Adam didn't wish anyone dead, he was perversely glad Micah was, the temptation to do the job himself might have proved irresistible. Collecting himself, Adam knew he had to get this right, guessing he probably had only had one chance to convince her.

"Daisy, Micah was a moron. He obviously couldn't see or appreciate what was right in front of him. You are beautiful, sensual, caring, generous, and kind, and the way you react when I kiss you is anything but frigid. I find you incredibly sexy." He swept his hand over her stomach even so slight a caress eliciting a tremor. "See," he grinned when she shimmied against him, "but I digress. Daisy, I love you. I — *we* — have Molly. Together you two enrich my life, complete my world, and fill my heart. I ache that you cannot bear a child of your body, but should you take a chance on me, and we decide to add to our family, we can consider adoption. Daisy, my greatest desire is to marry you, I want to show you how much I love you every day for the rest of my life. I want you to be Molly's mother — she already loves you as one — and I want the three of us to be a family. I know I'm not being very clear but—"

Adam wasn't allowed to finish his rather convoluted entreaty. Daisy cupped his face in her hands, kissing him until he thought the sun had exploded.

"I love you, Adam Willoughby. I never thought I could love anyone the way I love you. Thank you for saving me, for believing in me and for making me whole again. I know we are going way too fast, but I don't care, I never want to let you go." Echoing Adam's heartfelt wish, Daisy sealed their fate.

The rest of the afternoon spun and melded into a memory they would cherish for a lifetime.

Adam was right… Capri was a *very* special place!

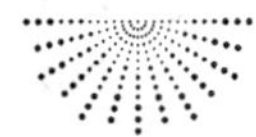

hree Months Later

Italy was shivering through one of the coldest Februarys on record, but the couple standing in the frosty courtyard of a hotel nestled along the Bay of Naples seemed unaware. Strains of classical music drifted across the chill air while Adam and Daisy exchanged their vows.

The bride, radiant in a winter-white gown, her flaming mop of curls spilling down her back — reminiscent of a lava flow from nearby Vesuvius — stood proudly beside her devastatingly handsome groom. The latter was attired in a dark charcoal suit, the green of his tie matching his new wife's sparkling eyes. Their diminutive bridesmaid — who chose turquoise for her dress and looked like a little princess — quite unashamedly, stole the show.

The previous three months had flown. Accompanied by Adam and Molly, Daisy returned to England, briefly, to settle her affairs. Upon meeting Adam, Reagan — who had travelled to Italy for the wedding — declared him utterly perfect, overjoyed for her best friend. Several specialist appointments, and more scans, concluded Daisy's spinal swelling had all but dissipated, her mobility increasing daily. Still not back to normal fitness levels and, occasionally requiring her wheelchair, for the most part Daisy managed with just a stick for support. She continued to work on her muscle strength with exercise and remedial massage therapy, hoping soon even that would be a thing of the past. Her nightmares were fading, and, to her everlasting relief, the sound of screaming metal rarely haunted her.

When asked whether she minded they marry, Molly was ecstatic, pleading to be allowed to call Daisy 'Mummy' immediately, effectively dousing Daisy's niggling concern she was coming between father and daughter.

The couple requested, and were granted, permission to marry at the hotel where Daisy stayed, and whose staff had been unfailingly kind. It was a simple ceremony, and the hotel manager put on a sumptuous wedding breakfast as a gift. The couple would be honeymooning at home, neither wanted to be away from Molly, and Daisy didn't care where she was as long as she was with Adam. A sentiment with which, her new husband reciprocated, wholeheartedly.

As the afternoon waned, Daisy glanced around the table, realising how lucky she was. She could never have imagined this time last year what she about to face, but she *had* faced it, and survived. Life chucked some pretty crappy obstacles at her and she overcame each one; maybe not very elegantly or gracefully but she'd done it. She reached for Adam, loving the gentle smile curving his oh so kissable lips, as he engulfed her hand in his.

Her heart thudded. Molly was staying at the hotel with Reagan for couple of days, giving the newlyweds time alone, and suddenly, Daisy needed her husband.

"Adam…" she whispered, her eyes holding his, darkening as the passion, never far away, began to burn, her gaze — a wish, a hope and a desire. Adam, oblivious to everyone around them, drew her close, kissing her deeply, his lips — a caress, a promise and a lifetime. Ignoring Daisy's squeaked protests, Adam swung his wife into his arms, thanking everyone, before striding out to where a car awaited their departure.

The car whisked them away into the start of their life together, and Adam continued that heady kiss.

As the world around them faded into insignificance, Daisy remembered that first step.

Who could have imagined where just one step would lead!

Rosie Chapel lives in Perth, Australia with her hubby and three furkids. When not writing, she loves catching up with friends, burying herself in a book (or three), discovering the wonders of Western Australia, or — and the best — a quiet evening at home with her husband, enjoying a glass of wine and a movie.

Website: www.rosiechapel.com
Facebook: https://www.facebook.com/RosieChapel-TheAuthor/
Twitter: @RosieChapel2015
Goodreads: https://www.goodreads.com/author/show/14759605.Rosie_Chapel
Amazon Author Page:
USA link: http://buff.ly/2jh0dgp
UK link: http://buff.ly/2jh2ND4

For your further enjoyment — I hope — I have included a chapter from Prelude to Fate, after which you can find synopses of my other books.

PRELUDE TO FATE

EMERITA AUGUSTA AD 37

The noise was deafening, the roar of hundreds, maybe thousands of people boomed around her. Where was she? Her mind wouldn't focus, everything was hazy, and the cacophony made it worse. Aghast, she became aware she was tied to something and a deadly foreboding ratcheted through her. She struggled to free herself, but the movement exacerbated her dizziness worse and, unable to help it, she vomited. Cackles of laughter reached her. Why were they laughing? What was going on?

Taking several deep breaths, she tried to concentrate, slowly opening her eyes onto the most terrifying sight of her life. She was in the arena, not in the seating area — actually *inside* the arena. A horrified moan fell from her lips as she looked around. There were several others in the same state of incapacitation as she. What was happening?

Desperately searching her mind for the explanation, she came upon a blank. She recalled being in her home — well, it was more a shelter really — on the edge of the town just inside the forest and away from prying eyes. The thunder of horses' hooves, the sounds of men shouting, her friends screaming, metal clashing. Peering out through the flap she saw three men coming towards her, and she had no chance of escape. A harsh voice yelled something at her in a tongue she recognised but his words made no sense, then nothing.

The Romans! That was who had done this to her, those *bloody* Romans. She thought herself safe; she lived on her own, away from the rest of the Vettones, on the perimeter of everything. She made enough coin to feed herself by selling woven cloth in the town. She created beautiful pieces and all the ladies of high status wanted her wares. She was always busy, she kept out of trouble and she did nothing to call the wrath of the Romans down on her head. So how the hell had she ended up here?

The hot sun was high above; it must be around the sixth hour. She was tied to a stake in the arena at midday. That could only mean one thing. Executions! Biting off a crude profanity, she attempted to gather her scattered wits, but her head throbbed, and everything remained fuzzy. Pushing herself upright, she stared across the huge circular space. The ground beneath her feet was covered in sand — the better to soak up the blood she presumed, cynically. Odd rock formations were spread around the arena and she could see some people shackled to chains pinned to these rocks, and there were others, like her, tied to wooden stakes. All looked demoralised, heads sagging, and clothes shredded. She glanced down and to her undying shame, noticed her own dress was ripped and barely covered her thin body.

Her humiliation was complete.

The roar went on unabated but as she listened, out of the random bawling came a sort of chant, whatever was going to happen was about to start. A strange smell began to permeate the air and suddenly she knew what she was about to face — a pack of wild animals. She inhaled deeply, detecting wolf and bear, maybe boar, at which point she knew she was doomed.

She knew what the Romans did, how they loved to watch people being torn limb from limb by starving animals. Even with her gift — the gift she kept so well hidden in dread of precisely this kind of situation — she did not think she would be able to stop animals driven to madness by lack of food. Distractedly, she wished she was still unconscious, that way she would not know what was happening until it was too late.

Tears began to roll down her cheeks, what had she ever done to deserve this?

A tall man leaned against the cool stone at the entrance to the arena. He hated these spectacles but as a veteran soldier he was included in the company of men tasked with keeping the peace. Keeping the peace on a day like this? Ridiculous! The morning bouts had been fairly tame, a few injuries but no deaths. This, the lunchtime *entertainment* never failed to turn his stomach. It was all very well killing on a battlefield, generally both sides had an equal chance to fight, they had weapons, tactics, and, for the most part, their numbers were balanced. Even gladiatorial combat had its place, participants carefully matched to give both a fair chance. Shackling people to rocks or posts was not balanced or fair, it was barbaric and, to the veteran, worse than any crime committed by the victims, some of whom were not criminals — just anti-Rome.

Sickened, he was about to turn away when he noticed a small figure at the far side of the arena. Blinking to make sure he wasn't imagining things, he recognised Lucia, the girl who sold those glorious pieces of cloth. He had purchased one for his mother. Shock hit him like a punch to the gut. This could not be right. What had she done to warrant such treatment? Rushing around to where the *lanista* — the manager of the Gladiators' School — stood with his charges, the man barked a question.

"From where did you acquire these miscreants?"

"Ah, Gaius Rufius, good day to you. They were rounded up out at the forest this morning. A patrol came upon them and, because they are known to be part of a subversive faction, they were brought in. It was no more than good timing that we already had an execution planned for today's event," Marcellus Aculeo, the lanista, replied.

"In that case how do you know they are guilty? There has been no trial. Have we stooped to executing people on the possibility that they might be engaging in seditious behaviour now?" Rufius was perplexed, this did not sound right at all. Fair enough, most criminals never really had a proper trial, but it seemed rather precipitous to snatch a group of people, and immediately have them killed without offering any chance to explain or defend their actions to their accusers.

Marcellus shrugged, "It is not my job to question the Watch, Rufius. These malcontents were brought to me, and because the games already included an execution, I simply boosted the numbers. It adds to the enjoyment of the crowd, and I fail to understand why this bothers you."

"You think that slip of a girl is a malcontent, a subversive?" Rufius spluttered, incensed, nodding towards Lucia. "She weaves cloth. From what I have heard, she lives on her own and has never shown any sign of being seditious. You must release her."

The greying lanista shook his head. "Too late, Rufius, the animals are about to be freed. Anyway, what is one less Vettone? They are no loss."

Rufius gawked at the man; stunned he could dismiss life so callously. All the more inexplicable because Rufius knew Marcellus had seen battle also. Most men, certainly those over the age of thirty, in Emerita Augusta were either soldiers on active duty, or veterans. To kill without reason seemed iniquitous and made them as culpable as the criminals in the arena.

"Surely someone has time to save her?" Rufius countered. "It will take mere seconds to get her out. I agree some have been causing trouble, but to let a young girl die for no other reason than it is easier than saving her is beneath us."

"Why do you care so much?" Marcellus asked curiously, "she is nothing to you."

"She is a person, and an innocent person at that; an artist who creates the extraordinary from the mundane, adding a little colour to our humdrum lives. She is well known in the markets, and respected for her work ethic; besides, she is scarcely more than a child. Does she sound like someone who is part of a rebel group?"

"Too late, Rufius," Marcellus repeated. "Forget her, she will be dead before you have time to think about it." As the lanista spoke, the roar from the crowd would have lifted the roof, had one covered the amphitheatre. Rufius could not believe it. He started to run into the arena but several guards — at a shout from Marcellus — stopped him, gripping his arms, and holding him against the chilled stone of the tunnel.

Rufius let loose with a string of expletives, calling into question Marcellus' family, his heritage and his legitimacy, which didn't bother Marcellus one jot.

In the meantime, Lucia, almost fainting from terror, frantically tried to break her bonds. It was hopeless, they were too tight. Whoever secured her to this post made sure there was no possibility of a last minute escape. The noise from the crowd reached hysterical levels as a pack of emaciated wolves slunk into the amphitheatre, snarling and drooling. Lucia bit back a despairing wail, and the ground seemed to pitch and roll, fear overwhelming her. The creatures paused, getting their bearings, sniffing the air, inhaling the scent of their wretched victims. Slowly, they padded towards those prisoners closest to the *fossa bestiaria* — the enclosure from where animals were released into the arena.

Immediately the wolves moved away from the fossa, three bears were loosed, followed shortly thereafter by half a dozen or so wild boar. Lucia was sobbing now. To see your own death, to look into the eyes of the crazed beasts who would inflict that death was a savagery she would not wish on her most hated enemy. Neither, in her worst nightmares, could she have imagined it would be she who faced such a death.

Blood-curdling screams rent the air as the so-called entertainment began in earnest. Lucia was one of the furthest from the fossa and witnessed the trauma of those taken down before her, the beasts circling closer and closer. She would never forget the sounds; they would haunt her forever — suddenly realising her forever was less than half an hour.

Knowing she only had one chance, Lucia let everything fade out, forcing herself to focus solely on the animals. For as long as she could remember she had shared an affinity with wild creatures. Her own tribe thought her some kind of mystic or at least under the protection of a deity — although in view of her current predicament, that appeared unlikely. It was not that she could bend animals to her will, or converse with them in the recognised sense — as some believed her capable — more she seemed able to understand and soothe them If an animal was sick or hurt she was usually able to heal it; if any were beyond help, she could ease their passing.

Thrusting her fright aside, Lucia drew what she hoped was a calming breath, and cleared her head. The noise of the crowd became muted, as though she was hearing them from a vast distance. She stared out over the arena, silently calling the creatures to her side. The alpha female of the wolf pack — resisting the summons, lifted her head testing the air, a low growl rumbling through her. Lucia ignored it, reaching out with her mind. Her spirit connected with the bears and they dropped onto all fours, shambling towards her, at the same time as the boars stopped gouging at their prey — grunted, appeared to falter, and trotted meekly after the bears. Last came the wolves. The alpha, surrendering to Lucia's call, padded regally across the sand, followed by the rest of the pack, the juveniles nipping at each other — to them this was just a game.

Soon all surrounded Lucia.

A hush fell over the crowd. Their anticipation a tangible thing, the sudden quiet almost as deafening as their roars. Rufius held his breath, his head refusing to accept what his eyes were seeing, his gaze fixed on Lucia who seemed to grow taller, her bearing now proud rather than defeated. One by one, every single beast lay down, jaws caked with blood and flesh, panting a little from their exertions, but without aggression, and within seconds became as passive as lambs.

Lucia gasped, trembling with the effort. She had done it! She was not safe, she was not free, this was simply a reprieve, but for a moment she could breathe.

Rufius marched back to Marcellus. "The gods have smiled on Lucia, even the wolves lay down before her. Would you risk their wrath by killing her now?"

Marcellus was dumbfounded. Never in all his long years had he seen such a thing, and he was not prepared to anger the gods by flouting their very clear indication that Lucia should be allowed to live. "You must get the approval of the sponsor. If he agrees to her release, you will assume all responsibility for her?" the lanista demanded.

Rufius nodded. "I will take her into my home, and she will be under my protection, but you must give me your word she is free. You will not seek her out to try to finish what you started." Rufius pinned Marcellus with a fierce gaze. The lanista nodded, and the two clasped hands firmly and shook. A soldier's agreement was binding, if the sponsor agreed, Lucia was saved.

Taking every care, Rufius walked into the arena, raising his hand to keep the audience quiet. He paused for precious seconds making eye contact with Quintus Antonius Valerius; procurator, sponsor of today's games, and a man Rufius knew relatively well. While he waited, motionless, he hoped his judgement of the man was correct. The official inclined his head, a slight smile on his lips. Relief poured through Rufius, and he continued steadily, but with haste across the arena towards Lucia.

The animal handlers followed at a reasonable distance. If the beasts decided to attack, they would not linger to save any but themselves. As he neared Lucia, Rufius called her name softly. She swung her head in his direction, and Rufius noticed her face was expressionless, her eyes empty.

"Fear not, Lucia. I come to release you," he said quietly, hoping she understood him. "Are you able to keep your friends placid while I remove your bonds?"

She nodded, biting her lip as he approached with a healthy degree of caution. Coming around behind her, he sliced the twine from around her waist, wrists and ankles. The threads falling away, blood dripping from where the restraints had scored her skin. He could see she was trembling, but her mind held the animals quiescent. Rufius lifted her into his arms, presuming, correctly as it happened, her legs would likely buckle if she tried to walk from the arena. Lucia held herself stiffly at first, until they were into the tunnel from where the gladiators entered, at which point she relaxed her mind, relinquishing her control over the animals. Her head lolled against his shoulder and she knew no more.

Wolf, bear, and boar slowly got to their feet, shaking their heads as if waking from a trance. The alpha wolf went to the stake and sniffed, then she turned and walked to the centre, her yellow eyes scanning the arena. Once there, she stopped and lifting her magnificent head, bayed — a long mournful howl, the unearthly sound sending the hairs up on the backs of the necks of each member of the audience. Then, as though released from a spell, they continued with their killing spree.

The crowd erupted.

~

Prelude to Fate is available from Amazon

OTHER BOOKS BY ROSIE CHAPEL

Historical Fiction

The Hannah's Heirloom Sequence

The Pomegranate Tree - Hannah's Heirloom - Book One

Echoes of Stone and Fire - Hannah's Heirloom - Book Two

Embers of Destiny - Hannah's Heirloom - Book Three

Etched in Starlight - Hannah's Heirloom - Prequel

Hannah's Heirloom Trilogy - Compilation – e book only

Prelude to Fate

Regency Romances

Once Upon An Earl - Linen and Lace - Book One

To Unlock Her Heart - Linen and Lace - Book Two

Love on a Winter's Tide - Linen and Lace - Book Three

A Love Unquenchable - Linen and Lace - Book Four

A Hidden Rose - Linen and Lace - Book Five

The Daffodil Garden

His Fiery Hoyden - A Regency Novella

A Regency Duet

A Regency Christmas Double

Contemporary Romances

Of Ruins and Romance

All At Once It's You

Cobweb Dream

His Heart's Second Sigh

Anthologies

The Lady's Wager - For Melissa

Love Kindled - Building Love

Winning Emma - With Love From London - VOTH: Vol 1

A Love Impossible - With Love from Dublin – VOTH: Vol 3

Chasing Bluebells - Wicked Spawns A Legacy of Evil (Coming Soon)

A Guardian Unexpected – Unconditional (Coming Soon)

The Pomegranate Tree
Hannah's Heirloom ~ Book One

Hoping to trace the origins of an ancient ruby clasp, a gift from her long dead grandmother, Hannah Wilson travels to the fortress of Masada with her best friend, Max. Strange dreams concerning a rebel ambush begin to haunt Hannah and following a tragic accident, she slips into the world of Ancient Masada.

A woman out of time, Hannah must rely on her instincts and her knowledge of what will befall this citadel to survive. Will she escape, or is she doomed to die along with hundreds of others as Masada falls — and what does any of this have to do with an ancient ruby clasp?

Echoes of Stone and Fire
Hannah's Heirloom ~ Book Two

Pompeii - a vibrant city lost in time following the AD79 eruption of Vesuvius. Now rediscovered, archaeologists yearn for an opportunity to uncover the town's past. Some things, however, are best left alone - revealing the secrets hidden beneath the stones could prove perilous. Hannah and Max are brought to Pompeii by a surprise invitation to join an excavation team who are trying to uncover the city's long history.

After entering an excavated house that bears a Hebrew inscription, Hannah's two worlds collide, and she falls back through time to ancient Pompeii. A place where her ancestor is a physician to gladiators engaged in mortal combat, where riotous mobs run amok and where a ghost from the past returns to haunt her.

Will Hannah and her loved ones manage to escape the devastation she knows is coming, before the town is engulfed in volcanic ash? Will she ever find her way back to Max the love of her life, waiting not so patiently millennia away? Or will echoes be all that remain?

Embers of Destiny
Hannah's Heirloom ~ Book Three

AD80 ~ Hannah and Maxentius must embark on a new journey to Northern Britannia. This harsh frontier is far from the comforts of Rome and danger lurks where least expected; a garrison of soldiers, some unhappy with their isolated posting; local tribes, outwardly accepting of their Roman occupier, but who may still resent the seizure of their lands.

Millennia away, Hannah Vallier finds a familiar item while working in a museum near Hadrian's Wall. It is the pomegranate; carved by Maxentius on Masada. Before Hannah can discuss it with Max, disaster strikes! Believing her husband has been killed, Hannah retreats into the past, her soul melding with that of her ancestor, but with little idea of what they could face. Is the risk from the conquered tribes, or much closer to home?

As rebellion threatens to shatter a fragile peace, Hannah's heart whispers that just maybe Max isn't dead and that he is calling her home. Can she trust her heart, or will she remain caught out of time, her destiny floating away like embers on a breeze?

Etched in Starlight
Hannah's Heirloom ~ Prequel

Maxentius ~ a Roman soldier fresh from the battlefields of Armenia, arrives to take command of the military outpost of Masada, Herod's isolated citadel in the Judaean desert. A seemingly mundane posting after years of warfare, Maxentius finds it more challenging to maintain a focused garrison than to face the wrath of the Parthians across a disputed frontier.

Hannah ~ a young Hebrew physician spends her days dealing with injuries from street brawls, deprivation, disease and loss. As her beloved Jerusalem plunges into chaos; her brother — who belongs to a band of rebels determined to drive out their Roman occupiers — tells her of their plans to storm a desert fortress and steal the weapons stored there, persuading his reluctant sister to go with him.

Masada ~ following the ambush, Hannah finds and treats three badly wounded Roman soldiers. In the aftermath and against impossible odds, Hannah and Maxentius realise that they are more than healer and captive, their fate already etched in starlight.

Prelude to Fate

For Lucia, staring into the jaws of an horrific death, escape seems impossible.

Rufius Atellus, a veteran Roman soldier, is appalled when he recognises one of the victims about to be executed. Surely this is a ghastly mistake?

A ferocious she-wolf, anticipating a tasty meal, suddenly finds herself under a human's control.

In an unexpected twist, and as danger threatens, the lives of all three become inextricably entwined. Was it chance brought them together in that theatre of bloodshed, or simply a prelude to fate?

(NB: Although this is a standalone novel,
it is *very* loosely linked to the Hannah's Heirloom Sequence)

Once Upon An Earl
Linen and Lace ~ Book One

When Fate saw fit to intervene in the life of Giles Trevallier, the very respectable Earl of Winchester, by dropping a female — soaked to the skin and with no memory of who she is or how she came to be there — literally at his feet, no one could have predicted the outcome.

While uncovering her identity, Giles realises he is falling hopelessly in love with his mystery guest, who unbeknownst to him, is succumbing to similar emotions; but, when the heart is involved, a thoughtless word or gesture can thwart even Fate's best-laid plans.

Faced with misunderstandings, whispers of scandal, secret documents and foreign agents, their chance at a happy ever after seems elusive, but fairy tales often happen when least expected, and love — however inconvenient — usually finds a way to conquer all.

To Unlock Her Heart
Linen and Lace - Book Two

Abused by a duke, and shunned by Society, relief seems at hand when Grace Aldeburgh is bequeathed a house in a small village, far from malicious gossips.

Once there, a tentative friendship blooms between Grace and Theo Elliott, the local doctor, who has already resolved to be the man to unlock her heart.

Just when happiness appears to be within her grasp, her erstwhile tormentor once again stalks Grace. After a failed kidnap attempt, the duke's quest culminates in an acrimonious confrontation, and the reason for his venal pursuit becomes agonisingly clear.

Love on a Winter's Tide
Linen and Lace ~ Book Three

Lady Helena Trevallier is in no hurry to marry, unwilling to allow a man to dictate her life. She has a secret, one that would probably horrify her social set and one any prospective suitor would demand she curtail. Every day, Helena disappears into a world few acknowledge, helping the poor, downtrodden and abused.

Hugh Drummond avoids most of the Society events he is invited to; events stalked by mamas seeking husbands for their daughters. A state of wedded bliss is something that holds no interest for him. Busy managing his shipping line, he sees no need for a wife, whose only joy is dancing and frivolity. If — and it was a huge if — he ever married, he would want a woman as capable as he, not some giddy society Miss.

Then, Hugh meets Helena and despite their resolve, fate, it seems, has other ideas. As their attraction deepens however, treachery threatens to tear them apart. Will they uncover the perpetrator in time, or will their love be swept away, lost forever on a winter's tide?

A Love Unquenchable

Jessica Drummond, a bright and cheerful young woman, rarely gives romance, let alone love, a thought. Long hours working in her brother's shipping office affords little chance of her ever meeting an eligible bachelor.

Duncan Barrington, veteran of the Napoleonic Wars, believes himself wounded in both body and soul. He has no intention of inflicting his demons on anyone, certainly not a beautiful and, in his opinion, irresponsible city lady.

One cold and snowy morning, the plight of a bedraggled puppy throws Jessica and Duncan together and, as a spark of something indefinable yet wholly unquenchable begins to burn, it is unclear who rescued whom.

A Hidden Rose
Linen and Lace ~ Book Five

After witnessing his mother's grief at the loss of his father, Nick Drummond resolved never to cause someone he loved such distress. Even the happiness of his siblings would not sway him – until he met Rose.

Rose Archer was almost content assisting her doctor father in a tiny fishing village in the north of Yorkshire. To experience the world beyond, a tantalising dream – until she met Nick.

Unexpectedly, the impossible becomes possible, and the renounced – desired above all things, but the shipwreck that brought them together, may yet tear them apart. Will Nick learn to trust his heart, or will his love for Rose remain forever hidden?

The Daffodil Garden
A Regency Romance

Horrifically scarred during the war, William Harcourt - Marquis of Blackthorne - prefers to spend his days in the quiet of his daffodil garden; plants do not pity, turn away, or judge.

Lucy Truscott, whose life is far removed from that of the ton, has no idea that by saving the life of a young woman, to whom she bears an uncanny resemblance, her own will be placed in mortal danger.

A chance encounter leads to something more. William begins to trust that Lucy sees the man beneath the scars, while Lucy is persuaded that love might actually transcend status.

Unfortunately, before their courtship has really begun, someone has every intention of ending it - permanently.

~

His Fiery Hoyden
A Regency Novella

A plea for help ignored. A child left to bring up her baby brother.

Livvy has no respect for the nobility; they let her down when she most needed them. Why should she accede to their demands now?

Philip, Lord Harrington, is stunned to discover the young heir to the dukedom lives a stone's throw away in a ramshackle cottage, and resolves to restore the child to his birthright.

They meet in a clash of wills, but just when it seems Livvy might surrender, the victory Philip desires, may not taste all that sweet.

~

A Regency Duet

Luck be a Pirate
(first published in the Kiss My Luck Anthology)

Luck wasn't something retired pirate Kennet Alexson believed in – good or bad. However, even he had to concede that landing a job at Trentams shipyard, and meeting Lynette Collins, was more than coincidence.

Fortune it seemed, was smiling on him for once.

As Kennet adjusts to life on dry land, his friendship with Lynette deepens into something far more enduring, and what once seemed elusive now becomes possible.

Unfortunately, fate has other plans, and Kennet's good luck is about to run out.

The Highwayman's Kiss
(first published in the Once Upon a Love Anthology)

Nothing exciting had ever happened to Juliette St Clair. Her days were spent assisting her father or calling on friends, wandering art galleries, taking constitutionals or, and more preferably, escaping into her books. Her evenings her evenings — an endless round of balls, where she preferred to remain invisible.

Until the day she was robbed by a highwayman.

A Regency Christmas Double

Heart Rescued
(originally published in the Tales for the Season Anthology)

Four years since Jasper lost the woman he was hoping to marry. Four years since he closed his heart and withdrew from Society. He has no idea his reclusive existence is about to be shattered.

Enter his sister's best friend, Harriet, a flame haired beauty, who needs his help.

Reluctantly he agrees and as they spend time together, it is clear their feelings run deep.

Although Harriet affects Jasper in a way no woman ever has, he believes her to be out of his league ~ but it's Christmas and she might just be the one to melt his frozen heart

Catch a Snowflake

Romance often blossoms in the most unlikely of places - but in a ward full of wounded soldiers - surely not?

When Lucas Withers comes face to face with Jemima Parsons - a young woman who blames him for her brother's injury - falling in love is the last thing on their minds.

What neither of them anticipated, was the magic of snowflakes.

~

Fate is Curious

Happily, ever after? No such thing! Bereft, following her beloved husband's sudden death, Lady Charlotte Sherbrooke has lost her belief in such romantic nonsense.

Successful shipping merchant, Zacharie Romain, is no stranger to loss; his business can be hazardous. Moreover, his wife died in childbirth and even though it happened a decade ago, he has no mind to expose himself to such sorrow again.

They meet in less than joyful circumstances but, as the year turns and grief diminishes, the woes of a small boy become the catalyst for something wholly unexpected. Can Charlotte and Zacharie trust what Fate has in store or will past heartbreak prevent them from taking a chance on love?

Of Ruins and Romance

Kassandra Winters has intrigued Gabriel St Germain since he accidentally knocked her flying outside her university professor's office. Her face haunts his dreams, yet he never expected to see her again. So, he is surprised when she appears, as though destined to do so, in the middle of a ruin, and he concocts a plan to win her heart.

Gabriel's old-fashioned courtship touches something deep inside Kassie and, although struggling to believe someone as handsome as Gabriel could possibly be interested in her, she soon realises she has fallen irrevocably in love with him. However, just as Kassie shares everything of herself with Gabriel, her world comes crashing down.

Can their romance survive, or will it fall in ruins, like the relics of antiquity that brought them together?

All At Once It's You

When Alex arrives in the small village of Rosedale Abbey, to take up a position as a research assistant for a renowned archaeologist, the last thing she is looking for, or expects to find, is love.

Jake was perfectly happy with the status quo. When it came to relationships, he didn't do committed or long term. He called the shots, and if his current flame didn't like it, she knew what to do. A philosophy, which served him well - until he met Alex.

Romance blooms, but even as the untamed wilderness of the North Yorkshire moors weaves its spell, a long-buried secret might yet jeopardise their happily ever after.

~

Cobweb Dreams

A holiday on the Scottish isle of Mull was just the break Chloe Shepherd needed, an escape from her boring office job and her complete lack of anything resembling a social life. Romance, it seems, isn't on the cards and, although Chloe dreams of finding her soulmate she is beginning to believe love is like cobwebs — spun overnight, only to vanish in the early morning breeze.

Under sufferance, Dominic Winters makes a flying visit to Mull to check on a rental property owned by his family. He hasn't got time for this — so indulging in a holiday fling is the last thing on his mind.

A lamb stuck in a bog proves a most unexpected match-maker and, while Mull weaves its magic, Chloe wonders whether those fragile cobwebs might be far more stubborn than she thought.

~

His Heart's Second Sigh

Reuben Faulkner and Paige Latimer are two happily single people, who have no desire to upset the status quo.

Unexpectedly, they are thrown together, only to discover both want far more than a casual friendship.

Just when things take an interesting turn, Reuben's past catches up with them, and threatens to derail their blossoming romance before it has chance to start.